MY ALIEN PRINCE

ROTHA MATES OF XAVIA | BOOK ONE

REVERIE HARWOOD

MY ALIEN PRINCE

ROTHA MATES OF XAVIA | BOOK ONE

REVERIE HARWOOD

Cover design by Mayhem Cover Creations
Editing by Epona Author Solutions

Copyright © 2023 Reverie Harwood
All rights reserved
ISBN-13: 978-1-950439-78-2

To my Universe of Possibility and Romance
and To Yours

Prologue

Katy

They called it 'getting left at the altar,' but in truth, we never actually made it down the aisle.

I had been in the bridal suite inside the church getting ready. I had most of my wedding dress on, because apparently that's how it worked. Sara, my sister, was stealing pieces of my bouquet to put into my hair as she pinned it up. I had paid someone to do my makeup, because I hadn't been confident enough to do it myself. The stylist had icy blue hair with tattoos and makeup just as bright and colorful. She flitted around the two of us, making me look flawlessly gorgeous. I wished I had her skills.

So yeah, after a while I got word; Mike hadn't been seen. Tyrone, his best friend and best man, who was supposed to drive him to the church hadn't shown up either. They wanted to know if I had heard from them. I texted and called, the same as everyone else, but this time *from the bride.* No answers. Mike's number went straight to voicemail, like his phone was off.

My mind, of course, went to the worst-case scenario—it's amazing how on such a wonderful day your thoughts can quickly go off the rails. I imagined their car in a ditch, and the guys hurt and being rushed to the hospital. I sent Mike's Dad to check the route from the church to Mike's apartment.

Eventually, Tyrone showed up at the church, by himself. This was about the time the ceremony should have started. By this time everyone knew the groom was late. They said no one had ever seen Tyrone's large mass move so quickly as it did from the entrance of the church building, up the stairs to the suite. He hadn't wanted to answer any more questions than required. He entered the bridal suite and told me what his cowardly friend couldn't tell me himself.

Mike wouldn't be coming today.

Tyrone's a big guy, but I could see he was ready to get beat down by me, definitely Sara, and possibly the rest of the bridal party. By that time, it was just me and Sara in the suite, though. I had sent the rest of the party out of the room, because I couldn't handle everyone's looks of concern. The makeup artist had left, but maybe she shouldn't have, because rivulets of tears began smearing the makeup down my cheeks.

"Is that all you came to say?" I choked out, noticing he had absolutely no words of explanation.

"Uh, yes," he said, remaining still, physically accepting the possibility of becoming some sort of punching bag. He was still in the remnants of his suit, trousers, white button-down. He'd lost his jacket; his tie was sticking out of his pocket. At least it had been a last-minute decision? That's the only thought that brought me any sort of clues, because they weren't coming from Tyrone.

I hadn't wanted them from Tyrone anyway. I wanted them from Mike, and he obviously wasn't going to arrive or tell anyone anything. Not me. Not his friends. Not his family. He had left me here to clean up this entire mess.

So yeah, they called it being left at the altar, but I didn't even make it down the aisle. I had the strange desire to run away, too, without a word. Like people would maybe decide we had both gotten cold feet and took off in mutually separate directions. But really, I was there. And if he had been, I would have married him.

And it would've been the happiest day of my life.

Sara cleaned everything up for me. I was thankful to her for that. She allowed me to sit in the bridal suite in shock while she made all the decisions, all the announcements, ushered everyone and their questions away. I don't even know half of what was decided that day. Somehow the presents were sent back to their recipients.

Later, I received some sympathy cards, which was weird, but I guess made sense if you were there to witness the train wreck.

"At least he didn't marry you," was a phrase I was told a lot by friends.

It was a strange consolation—not being married. That after all the omissions, the lies, the lead-up that brought me to the threshold of a forever-life, at least he had stopped short of the written contract, had stopped short of opening the wedding presents (made it easier to return them), had stopped short of getting that free upgrade for the honeymoon suite.

I had worried for a long time that I had pushed Mike too much. I had been one of those women with her dream wedding in her back pocket. I couldn't help it; I was a wedding photographer. I've been to countless weddings. Of course, I had thought about my own. Weddings hadn't really been his thing, and I'd been OK with that. Weddings were an event, a party, a celebration. It was completely different from the actual marriage. I clearly hadn't understood though, because obviously, weddings *really* weren't his thing. Then why had he asked me to marry him?

I hadn't made that up. I hadn't pushed him into it. I truly thought he'd wanted to spend his entire life with me. Weddings were one day. Marriages were for the long-haul. I had been ready for that. I understood we'd have fights. I understood that even the best relationships could fail, but he hadn't bothered to try. I didn't even know if he'd never wanted to try, or if he'd changed his mind, because we never talked after our failed wedding. I never got answers.

That's right. I hadn't talked to him since, and he never tried to contact me. Maybe he thought I was mad and didn't want to talk to him, that I didn't care about his reasons. That wasn't the case. Of course, I wanted to know why he left. That was probably what hurt the most.

Actually, one year later and that wasn't what hurt the most anymore. What hurt the most now was my wallet. It would be one thing to lose deposits if the event was canceled. I was a wedding photographer. I was in the business. If there was a chance I could rebook for that day, I usually gave the client their deposit back. Obviously, I get it, even more now. And even if you don't get all your deposits back—they were at least only partial payments—half at the very most. That's half you get to keep if things fall through.

But for me and him—it wasn't just deposits. It was the whole day, the whole event, the catering, the everything. Nothing was canceled. It was all paid for, and it was all provided. I'm not sure if Sara sent the guests home with their dinners or if it was sent to the local homeless shelter. I didn't deal with it; I hadn't asked. But the idea was that the event and all the services were provided, I just didn't get married.

And as much as my sister yelled at me all the time for it, I refused to go chasing after him. I had been the one who wanted the fancy wedding. I'd been the one who had signed all the papers, had bought things on credit—sure, I thought we were going to be paying it back together, but it had been me who had done it, all the same. Sara thought I was punishing myself for not knowing that he was going to ditch me. Maybe I was hurting myself, but I refused to seek out someone who didn't want to be sought. I wasn't going to camp on his doorstep for an explanation, for an apology, and absolutely nothing as basic as money. If he wasn't going to say anything, neither would I.

I would have rather drowned in my debt.

…I was in so much debt.

You thought I'd be able to just go back to work? Photographing all the beautiful brides on their wedding days where their handsome, if a bit clueless, grooms actually showed up?

Yeah, even if I thought it was going to work that way, it didn't work that way. Mike managed to mess up more than one type of future for me. After helping my immediate clients book with other photographers, I hired a couple of assistants, but without me actually taking the photos, it was a lost cause. I wasn't going to be able to make any money that way.

I was in debt and didn't have any clear way to get out of it.

My sister, however, thought she had the answer.

Chapter One
The Tropical Paradise of Xavia

Katy

Sara and I were having one of our usual movie-and-popcorn nights, this time at my apartment. I was in the kitchen, making two batches of popcorn—one salty and buttery, and the other kettle corn, my favorite. I liked both, so when we were at my place, we had both. Sara sat on the couch, her back to me, picking out the movie, which meant that we were going to watch something hilarious and ridiculous. She always picked out the best movies. I poured us giant glasses of white wine, because that went with popcorn, right? Sure.

"When is your lease up here?" she asked over her shoulder.

"Not soon enough." In the wake of the Mike-pocalypse, I renewed my lease so I'd have somewhere to live. It had been a terrible financial mistake. I had considered getting a roommate, but there was only one bedroom. Now, I was just waiting for the lease to end again, so I could move some place more affordable.

Sara stopped scrolling through the movie list on the screen. She turned, kneeling on the couch cushion so she could face me. "And that's why you need to go to Xavia with me."

We had the same eyes. Our mom's hazel eyes. Her hair was a darker brown than mine, like Dad's. Just a few years apart, we were closer than thieves. My little sister was the more rambunctious and rebellious one, but with all that I had gone through with Mike, she'd been by my side being more of a big sister and caretaker than anything else. It was sweet to see that side of her, but I also felt a bit guilty about it. I was the big sister. I was the one supposed to be taking care of her.

And that's why I really wished she would drop this whole *Xavia thing*.

Xavia was the newest pamphlet planet being promoted by the American government. They wanted us to think it was a skipping stone's throw away. And maybe it was now with the technology they'd purchased from the Arqal. Faster than light travel was now possible, and of course, the government was using it to promote vacations and even, brand new lives. Still, there was the time in stasis—months where something could go wrong, and you'd just be *gone*. My sister wasn't talking about visiting Europe, or even traipsing through the rainforest. She was talking about traveling across the galaxy.

Sara had fallen in love with Xavia as soon as she'd heard about it. The photos they showed made it look like Hawaii—tropical, lush, no winters. It was volcanic, I guess. It was mountainous. It wasn't just the scenery she enjoyed. The villages were full of good-looking men. They were surprisingly human-looking, after looking past their facial features and skin colors. Their villages were cobblestone and quaint, but we were assured they had plumbing, electricity, and advanced electronics. It did seem like a nice place to visit, but I was skeptical. To me, it looked like jungles just over the edges of the photos.

"It sounds like a giant government experiment to me," I complained. It was a complaint, because I had said it many times before. Maybe they were looking for volunteers to dump on a planet to 'see what happens.' We were still plenty overpopulated; maybe they just wanted some of us off this one.

"A paid experiment! Katy, go on this vacation with me. Six months—"

"—not including travel time." Three months in stasis, each way, doubling the time.

Sara ignored me. "All expenses paid. You'll be out of debt *and* you'll have a job. They want us to document our travels. You're a *photographer*."

She was already three-fourths through qualifying for the program. I didn't think she'd make it that far; else I would have stopped her from applying at all. But she was right, the government was paying people to visit, to show that space travel wasn't all that bad. They paid to keep your life in check here, and for me that would mean covering the expenses I was having trouble covering myself. They'd pay my rent or get me out of my lease, if I wanted. They'd be giving me money for my time, and buying my photos—goodness knows they needed them. They showed the same twelve all the time.

But still, I was no adventurer. My sister was the adventurer. It was partly my fault for not having nipped this in the bud and refusing to let her apply at all. Why did the government think she would make a good applicant/astronaut? She had already drunk half the glass of wine that was supposed to be for the movie. She hadn't even picked a movie. She was pretty set on talking me into this. And the problem was, she was right. I needed to do *something*. The finances were going to avalanche upon me in just a few weeks. I needed a solution.

"Let's say I do go…"

"Oh my gosh! Oh my gosh!" she jumped up and down on the couch on her knees. Her face completely brightened. She really did want me to go. "I've been telling the recruiter all about you. They're willing to accelerate your application."

"That doesn't mean they'll accept me."

"Of course, they'll accept you. You're the better version of me! Oh gosh, I hope they don't replace me. I hate you."

I laughed at her speedy line of logic, but I had spoken with her recruiter as well. I was pre-approved across several levels due to my biological relation to someone already partly through the program. I was glad, but also felt a little suspicious.

Did they just take anyone? At one time, astronauts were supposed to be some of the best our planet had to offer with the world's greatest training. And here, I felt like my sister got picked off an Instagram post she'd tagged #space-explore or #Xaviabound. I didn't know, but I wasn't going to let my sister visit an unknown planet without me. What sort of big sister would just let that happen?

"I can't believe we're going into space! And meeting hunky guys! This is just the re-start you need. This is going to be awesome."

Part of that was definitely right. I needed a fresh start. Xavia just might be it.

And if not, at least I'd be debt free. And I'd have some photographs I could sell instead of having to choke down the vomit that rose every time I thought about photographing another crap-tastic wedding.

I sipped my wine to settle the flutter in my stomach. "What movie are we watching?"

"Mars needs Moms," she said, immediately returning to her task at hand. Well, one hand. Her other held her empty glass. "Refill me, please?"

I laughed at her movie choice and refilled us both. We were going to need it.

Chapter Two
Waking from Stasis

Katy

Waking from stasis was the weirdest thing, and thankfully a private thing. What I had seen in science fiction movies where they're all in pods side-by-side, looking perfect and waking from some wonderful beauty sleep—yeah, there was none of that here. The first thing I noticed was my fingernails. I felt an itch on my arm, so I moved my hand to scratch it…and that must be why they secured our wrists. My hand didn't move and when I looked down my finger nails had grown freakishly long. Imagine if I'd try to scratch my eye.

We all had separate rooms with a stasis pod, toilet, sink, shower, cot, and television—although I didn't know when we'd use the last two. I tried to orient myself. I was secured to a pad inside the pod which was mostly upright. I hadn't felt like it had been that long, but definitely time had passed. And my nails were the first sign of that. I suddenly and immediately wanted to see a mirror. How much time had passed? How much had I aged? I couldn't believe I had let my sister talk me into this. And then, I thought of my sister. Goodness, where was she? Was she OK? Before I could freak out too much, the restraints released, and I was able to stumble gently out of the pod.

Next to the pod were some grooming tools. I immediately cut my nails, gross. So gross.

OK, that wasn't the grossest. The grossest was taking the catheters out of my body. Sure, it was great that I wasn't soiling myself in the pod, but…never mind, let's not talk about it.

After cleaning myself up, I dared to look into the mirror. I took it slowly. I didn't want to frighten myself.

And there I was.

My hair was longer and decently greasy. The stasis pods cleaned us to some extent, but the technology was far from perfect. I recognized my heart-shaped face. My nose was still a smidge too big, but there was more I didn't recognize. There were a couple more wrinkles. A bit of sag to my skin. Was it always like that? I hoped I just needed some water. Goodness, I was thirsty.

The freckles on my skin had faded, and I tried not to think about how far away from the sun…our sun… we were. We were, supposedly, somewhere entirely else.

I drank from the bottle of water sitting by the pod and felt my body completely revolt. The liquid felt so foreign in my body, in my mouth. I felt it going down my throat and changing my internal temperature. I may not have understood how much time had passed, but it was enough for my body to have forgotten what it was like to even drink water. That was insane.

This was insane.

What was I thinking letting my sister talk me into this?

I opened the door into the hallway. It was time to find Sara. She owed me one. A big one.

"Whoa! This is so cool! You are so old!" shouted my sister as she ran toward me. She had changed, too. It was like I'd fast-forwarded and things were just a bit off.

There were other women in the hallway, in varying stages of confusion and worry, but overall calm. I wondered if we'd been given drugs to help ease us into wakefulness. Why not? They had drugged us for everything else for months.

This must have been the female section of the ship. There were only females of similar age to me and my sister. That sort of made sense. Pick the healthiest, young ones—they'd be most likely to survive the trip. They'd also look great for the government pamphlets they had to sign photographic releases for.

"You guys know each other? Wait, are you sisters?" asked a woman with thick, jet-black hair. Her dark features on her olive, sandy skin made it look like she was already wearing evening makeup.

"Yep, anyone know when we're actually going to get off this ship?" Sara asked. "I need some time to…preen."

We all did. The stasis pods removed filth, but it just didn't feel the same as taking a shower. I felt like I had several days…ahem, months…of grime on me. I didn't want to think about it. I wasn't the only one that felt that way. I imagined others hadn't even bothered to venture out yet without that first shower. Maybe I should get in there before all the hot water was gone. Was there hot water?

There was hot water. And we were all able to take showers and clean off the layer of muck. In the shower, I began to feel a little panic. It worried me that there hadn't been any staff members to greet us when we woke. I noticed the woman with dark hair and features—Sophie—had discreetly checked doors and none of them opened. Had something gone wrong? Did we wake up too early, or too late?

Thankfully, that hadn't been the surprise.

The surprise came two hours later when we entered the atmosphere of the planet, Xavia, and a Welcome Video started in all of our rooms. Those in the hall rushed to the closest television. Sara and I sat on the cot in my room. Sophie and a red-headed girl who had introduced herself as Leah stood nearby.

"Welcome to Xavia, ladies," said the government official I recognized from the other educational videos. I noticed the gender-specific greeting. It was strange they'd made a video separately for the women. Maybe there were some cultural differences they wanted to touch on? They should have done that earlier.

"Thank you for participating in our cultural exchange mission. We have been very clear on the importance of this program, but not exactly clear on *how* it is important. You see, you have been chosen to save this planet in a genetic exchange. This planet has two important resources. One is holmium, known to us as a rare Earth metal. It's critical in all of our industries, space-travel, surface-travel, medical, communication, computers, defense. The second resource is the natives that maintain the mines. You are here for the second, their species is on the edge of collapse. They are lacking females, and your wombs are the only things that can save this species."

"Did he just say wombs? Oh my god," Leah whimpered.

We could hear shouts from the other rooms too. Sara grabbed me tight.

"Where is he? I'm going to tear him apart," said Sophie with an unsettlingly calm voice.

"Do you think there are any men on this ship?" I asked, now wondering if this wasn't just a female-hall, but a female ship.

"We will be back in one year, Earth-time, to see how you are all faring. We hope you can build connections with the natives and create some biological ties that will reinforce our relationship with them and, of course, the holmium we desperately need. You women have been chosen for a special mission. We depend on you."

"We were abducted and trafficked," said Leah.

"Don't say that," I said, desperate for it to not be true.

"We're going to be alien sex slaves," she confirmed.

"Not if I have anything to say about it," said Sophie.

She started working the bolts securing the cot to the ship. I guessed she was trying to dismantle it to make a weapon. I thought about the personal belongings I was allowed. I had my camera gear and some movies. I was woefully unprepared for what Sophie was proposing.

Then the ship jostled and landed hard without warning. All of us were now on our butts or sides on the ground.

We had arrived on Xavia, and we had no idea what was waiting for us on the other side of the ship's doors.

Chapter Three
The Arrival

Drex

"You look tired, friend," said Vance. Vance was being kind. I was sure I looked like crap. He wrapped thick arms around my frame, jovially. His shaggy brown hair brushed my face. "At least put a smile on," he said with a bright-white toothy grin of his own. The color contrasted his lips and other light blue-green features.

Vance was right. He was almost always right, which was why he was my most trusted adviser. I smiled and tried to look less tired. I couldn't help it. My nervousness was paling my turquoise skin, making me look sickly. The stress was exhausting me.

I think I would have been a fine leader during times of peace. I wasn't one to go crazy with power. I would've followed the traditions of my people, and our history would only mention my name in passing. That would have been just fine for me. Instead, the stars had set me to rule during a time of complete uncertainty. There was no precedent for being a generation removed from tragic population decimation. There was little precedent for intergalactic affairs. I had been thrust into historical significance, and I was making it up as I went. I had to.

The Orkain were the bane of the Xavians. They must have arrived on ship, but we had never sighted it. The creatures were bodily about our size, and had horns, two eyes, a mouth, and Xavian-like torso and arms, but that's where the similarities ended. Their horns grew straight up. Their eyes were bright red. They had fangs, beast-like legs, and expansive wings. Their language sounded like the screeches and howls of animals, and they played the role well. They hunted at night, swooping down on Xavians, and carrying them off. We speculated they lived in the northern caves, but we hadn't been able to re-con. Instead, we busied ourselves creating new, protective homes for the remaining survivors.

My parents, King and Queen of Xavia, met the Orkain invasion with bravery and grace. They also met their own demises in the invasion and left me to pick up the pieces. I had at least met another alien species who were much less murderous. The Earthling humans were much like us, and seemed to be on a similar technological path as us—however, the first group of aliens they met hadn't devoured their female population. The Arqal introduced them to interstellar travel. And with my ahem, intergalactic prowess, I had been able to pioneer an interesting relationship between the humans and us. It wasn't overstating it, to say that Earthling humans could be Xavia's saviors simply by helping us continue our genetic lines.

The human ship was supposed to land today. Everyone knew it. And as much as I hadn't wanted us to gather, ceremony and circumstance argued for it. And I couldn't tell my people this was our new hope while at the same time denying exactly what made our people, us—and that was gathering and celebrating. We would keep it simple. We would take precautions. And we would disperse immediately. Besides Vance and me, there were the other twenty-eight men who would be hosting the women, twelve or so curious onlookers, and the five women I had asked to join us.

It wasn't just the dangerous mass gathering of my people that was stressing me out. I was also simply tired because I'd spent most of last night lying outside in the tall, cool grass above my home, staring into the sky, looking for the ship. The exact time of the ship's arrival wasn't something known or, at the very least, hadn't been communicated to us. It'd been months since we'd last talked to anyone from Earth. For the people on the ship, it would feel like less time, but they'd still age. Stasis and time-travel were still confusing to me. I tried not to think too hard about it. Instead, I watched for anything shooting among the stars and planets I'd come more and more familiar with, as I spent much of my time now as leader of our people, staring up for wisdom that I was probably too young and too small to understand.

It seemed impossible that creatures from so far away would be able to interact with us on such an intimate level, but their scientists and my scientists seemed to agree that despite some differences at all levels, the differences were small. Being a bit squeamish, I didn't ask them to elaborate. Leaders were about the um, bigger picture. And truly, the results were not as definite or specific as you'd think scientific reports would be. It summed up to, "We won't know until we know."

So now, with some amount of hope against hope, I was looking into the deep purple sky waiting for a moving, blinking light that would bring hope to our population that otherwise was projected to die out within the next two generations. Even if biological babies between us weren't possible, the introduction of humans, new personalities, and new femininity might just make *this* population and *this* generation hopeful enough to continue as well as they can, for as long as they can.

I was thankful to the yellowish-skin humans for that much. They had signed up, been put under some strange, risky sleep and sent across the galaxy to speak to us and get to know us. I would be eternally grateful for their bravery and curiosity. And despite that, I didn't want to be directly part of the program. I argued with Vance over it, and, of course, I'd lost. If I wanted anyone to have faith in the matching, I'd have to have faith in it myself. So, now, along with all my other princely duties, I would be hosting a human woman and bringing her into my home.

The chances were slim. The way my parents chose each other—glorious, spiritual, and biological rotha—was nearly impossible. There was no way *that* was on the ship for me. But, at the very least, maybe some of the matches from the ship would find happiness. I spent time trying to imagine what that world would look like, with happy couples—with me, as part of a happy couple. Thoughts of swooping Orkain invaded, tearing families apart. I tried to hope against hope.

So yeah, that's why I was tired.

Vance, a prime good-looking example of our species, had of course signed up to host one of the women, too. The Orkain had inspired our generation to grow strong, not only to fight the Orkain, but with so few women left, competition was fierce. A Xavian couldn't go solely off their personality or funny jokes anymore. One needed to show they'd be able to defeat an Orkain, protect his woman, protect his family. "Jokes are useless if a woman can't bounce a berry off your pecs," Vance would say while we worked together. It was also from a practical sense. Almost all the men had spent time doing some manual labor, even royalty, building new homes that would hide and protect us from the flying Orkain. We returned to mining metals as well—to trade with our new partners.

Vance had a big smile and an even bigger personality. He was also loyal, fair, and smart. I lucked out, because I could have easily found a best friend who would have led me astray, but at this point, it seemed Vance could have been the prince and I, the bad influence, that had led him astray in childhood. As of now, we were both thrust into these positions, mine because of my family's royal legacy and untimely death. His because of his constant connection to me and his loyalty to his people. If any woman were to fall for anyone, it would be for Vance. He deserved it too. He had a woman he had been crushing on when they were still in schooling, too young to experience rotha, but hopeful for it. That woman was now gone. One of the first to have been snatched away. Vance never talked about it because it had never been an official thing between them, but I knew better. Vance hurt, and he deserved better. Me? There hadn't been anyone, which was to my benefit, because it meant I hadn't lost them. Still, I had experienced the loss of my parents and hundreds of Xavians that had been under my care.

After even the most excited of us were starting to calm down, we recognized the ship as a large speck far in the sky, like a bright star or moon during the daytime. It flew by a couple of times in orbit, but didn't get any closer. Was it not going to land? Eventually something even smaller came into focus. The ship had deployed an object which landed in the jungles near us. We trekked there as quickly as possible, urged on by curiosity and also worry that the landing had attracted the Orkain.

Just as we arrived, the door opened and a ramp fell to the ground with a thump.

"Hello!" I called out, using the English I had learned. "You've arrived on Xavia. Welcome! Is everyone OK?"

A frightened, soft, and gentle voice replied, "We're OK."

The crowd that had gathered cheered. It concerned me how many of us were out here. I sent Lowree and the other four women I'd requested into the ship. Even though the humans had volunteered to come, I didn't want them to feel threatened by a bunch of men swooping in, picking them up, and running back to their caves with them. That would be later, I hoped.

It wasn't long and also, *so very long,* before Lowree came out to speak with me. By then, even more people had gathered despite me asking them to disperse. There would be time to meet all of the women and to get to know everyone, but for now, the group was too big, too tight, too warm. What Lowree had to tell me was so shocking though, that I quickly forgot about temperature dynamics and population safety—which was my fault. It all lay solely on me.

The women had been told this was a co-ed cultural exchange. They knew nothing about our population dynamics or problems. They hadn't even known they were all female until they landed here. They'd just been dropped off by their government for what...to be raped? Stars, I couldn't believe it. What sort of operation had I agreed to?

And then, the Orkain came.

Chapter Four
Welcome to Xavia

Katy

"Welcome to Xavia. We hope you show the men the best Earth has to offer. We are depending on you."

Leah cursed the officer out as the video faded and ended.

As if they knew we would hesitate to open the doors, what had appeared to be a wall in the hallway opened to the exterior of the ship where a ramp deployed. I hadn't noticed how sterile and quiet the ship had been until the door opened. We had been chattering and yelling, but it was not the same as the wickedly wild loudness of nature.

And it absolutely frightened me.

We all instinctively hunched and backed away from the door. It was like all preservation instincts had kicked in. Many of the women gripped scissors that had recently been used to cut hair, now held savagely in their hands as weapons.

The colors were bright and, admittedly, beautiful. Huge tropical plants could be seen from the door, along with a landscape that was lush, hilly, and wild.

"Hello!" shouted someone hesitantly from outside. English? Were we on Earth?

We stared at each other, confused. I couldn't see from my room, but it sounded like a group was gathering outside the ship. Perhaps this was all some sort of ridiculous practical joke. Perhaps we'd be shown the hidden cameras and be paid to sign off on some stupid television show.

"You've arrived on Xavia. Welcome! Is everyone OK?" tried the voice again. The longer sentence gave away that English wasn't their first language. It was a little broken, a little accented.

Since no one else was volunteering, I stood up and straightened my clean uniform—more to buy time than anything else—it wasn't like I was going to an interview. I wasn't much of a leader; I just wanted to find out what was happening so I'd best know how to protect my sister. I peered into the hallway.

"We're OK!" I said in my loudest, bravest voice.

There was an outburst of noise outside that confirmed there were many more men outside than just the one calling out. It was hard to understand if they were cheering or if they were angry. It was emotional, whatever it was. I cursed. No part of me wanted to go out there and find out, but I'd somehow taken point, and no one was about to swap with me.

I heard shuffling on the ramp. When they peered around the doorway, I knew immediately this was no practical joke.

These were aliens.

"Hay-rro," said the alien with a bit more 'r' than 'l.'

I immediately considered if I had only seen photographs of male Xavians. As this alien seemed to be the same species, but with some major differences.

I decided she might be female. Her skin was yellow-green and she didn't have any horns, only shorter textured ridges along her hairline. Her voice was higher pitched than the one that had called outside. Like the Xavians I had seen, her nose was flatter and with narrower slits than those of a human's. Unlike any of her friends, her face was framed with subtle sandy-brown irregular, curvy markings, like a cheetah's spots.

"I'm Katy," I said, and stepped into the hallway. "You speak English?"

"Yes, we're so excited for your arrival. We've all tried to learn your language so that you'd be more comfortable." The other women nodded, appreciatively. "The men sent us so that maybe you'd feel more comfortable."

I did feel…somewhat more comfortable. "So you are women? There *are* women here?"

"Yes, we're female." The woman gestured and four other women came in. Two appeared older by their darker and rougher skin texture, and thicker frames. All of them were beautiful with bright, clear eyes. The younger ones both had rounded stomachs. I wondered if they were pregnant. Maybe Earth had gotten it wrong. It seemed like they weren't having any trouble. The women here were absolutely stunning creatures, and suddenly I felt a lot safer being a plain Jane on Xavia. Maybe we didn't have anything to worry about.

The lead woman then gave a bit of a grimace. "I'm Lowree. We are some of the few females left."

So, it was true. The government had dropped us off to, what? Repopulate the planet?

With the five women in the hallway, it began to feel surprisingly warm. The women seemed to be radiating heat, even more than open threshold into the jungle. It was sort of comforting. Other women began to gather in the hall to meet the alien welcoming party. For women who had agreed to come to hang out on an alien planet for a year, they were shy. But I guessed the looming threat of alien slave trade had us suddenly cautious.

"Look, I'm not sure *what* you thought was going on, but we just got baited and switched here," said Sophie from behind me. She and Sara were hanging around the doorframe of my room.

"Baited and switched?" asked Lowree, hesitantly.

I tried to explain. "Our government told us that both men and women were coming on this journey to visit, and we would experience your culture. But then, we just saw a message from our government. They say they made a deal with you to um…copulate? Do you know that word?"

Lowree nodded.

Of course, she knew that word. Why *wouldn't* she have learned it? That's why they were there. The Xavians thought they were there for…copulation.

"They…baited and switched…lied to you? Dishonest?" said Lowree, looking at all the women who all shared the same desperate desire for this woman to understand their current panic and fear.

"Fryyre," muttered the woman. I didn't have to know the language to understand that it was a curse word. "Let me talk to the prince. You all can come if you like, but maybe it's best if everyone's intentions are made clear before they see you all. You all are…beautiful."

She had said it with the same awe that I felt about them. *They* were the gorgeous ones. I'm as pretty straight as they come, but even I was wondering if the men were anything like the women. Not that that's why I was here. I was curious, though.

The Xavian women stayed behind and spoke with those interested in speaking with them. I heard snippets of the Xavian language. It sounded rough and guttural—more Germanic than Spanish, although nothing like anything I'd ever heard.

Lowree returned, her composure gone.

"We have another problem. We have to go, NOW. The Orkain are coming."

Who?

She gestured for us to leave the ship. I would have hesitated, but the fear and panic in her voice sounded genuine and intense, and the other Xavians in the hall were just as quickened by the news. I emerged at the top of the ramp. The lush, bright jungle was now darkened by swirling clouds. The trees swayed, even though I couldn't feel the wind. *Something* was circling above us. Xavian men were on the ramp to escort us, but my eyes couldn't focus on them. On the ground, there were Xavians, scattering. I knew something was very wrong. I re-entered the ship and ran my hands along the threshold. There weren't any buttons or sensors—there was no way to close the door. My idiot-government was going to get its drop-off cargo killed. The only thing I could do was aid the Xavians in evacuating us.

I was one of the last women out—me, Sophie, and Sara. A strong hand wrapped easily and entirely around my arm. I typically would have been bothered by the touch of a stranger, but his skin was warm and smooth, and in stark contrast to the palpable fear in the air. He rushed me from the clearing where the spaceship had landed to the cover of the jungle's edge. My sister was being taken in a different direction by another man. I let out a shriek and pulled at the one who had my arm. Danger or not, I wasn't going to be separated from my sister. In the moment, I wasn't sure if my new distress registered with him at all. He was tall and built like a wall. Then, I was screaming in soundless terror, as a dark, winged demon dove down on me.

The Xavian pulled me close, picked me up, and sprinted into the jungle. Over his shoulder, I could see the creature stop short—a long tail steering him—and I got a good look at it. It was a deep, dark red and black, not like anything on the planet's landscape—no need for an apex predator to blend into the scenery, I guessed. It had a human torso and arms, and beastly, clawed legs, all of which seemed small and useless compared to its massive, feathered wing span. The horns on its head sprung outwards and up which made it look evil over the giant bug-like red eyes which covered half of his face. The horns matched in symmetry to its fangs which were the same shape but were pointed in the opposite direction, downward.

Soon my view was obscured by the thickness of the jungle, but I knew it was still out there. My heart thumped madly.

"What was that?" I screamed, shaking now that I'd been put down on my two feet. I half-expected him to shush me, but he didn't. I was torn between running back to find my sister, and not wanting to lead that thing to her. It had been looking right at me. At this point, it was probably safer to keep distance. There was only one of those creatures…right?

"It's an Orkain," he said in a level voice, finally looking at me. And honestly, he seemed a little surprised by me.

I guess I looked alien to him.

He looked alien to me.

The photos had made them look blue, but even in the shadows of the jungle, I could tell he was closer to turquoise with a glimmer that seemed to make his colors swirl on his skin. And there was a lot of skin—he was a big guy, and his large, muscular body was not hidden by his loose, half-open shirt. He was tall, maybe six and a half feet tall. He shared the small ridged bumps on his face like the women, but also had thicker black protrusions—horns, but unlike the demon's they grew along his face, framing its strong structure. It was difficult to see where the horns started and ended as they blended in with his equally dark, long hair.

His eyes were like ours, but not. Dark outlines along the lids, like he was wearing eyeliner…maybe he was, and the thinnest solid frame of color around huge irises that brightened with color and light, like a distant galaxy. They responded to mine, searched my face. I watched him focus on me; his eyes alight. The nervous pit that grew in my stomach and the buzz in my chest had nothing to do with the terrifying creature I'd just escaped from. This guy was mesmerizing.

A scream from the clearing broke our eye contact. Without thought except *Sara*, I rushed through to the tree line. Surprised by my direction, the Xavian missed grabbing me. He caught up quickly with me and pulled me back. I opened my mouth to protest, but the air caught in my throat as I saw the Orkain, taller than the entry to the spaceship he was leaving, with a human woman in tow. I tried slipping his grasp, but my alien grabbed my arm and flung me roughly into the foliage. He, and a couple other Xavians, launched from the tree line.

The Orkain had cleared the threshold, and could have taken off with its prey. Instead, it stepped down into the center of the clearing, as if it welcomed the challenge. It held the struggling woman in a tight bear hug, her feet off the ground. The group of Xavians lunged in some sort of formation. With a whip of its wings, it tossed them away as easily as my alien had done to me before he'd gone on the attack. With that show of force, the Orkain shoved off from its hocks and leaped into the sky, gone.

The Xavian returned to me, defeated, like there was nothing else to be done.

"What the hell," I said.

"What the hell?" he repeated, but as a question. He didn't understand.

"This is hell," I said, more to myself than to him. "Are you going to go save her? Fight it?" I asked. I couldn't imagine *not* going to rescue her, but they hadn't even brought weapons, even knowing that thing existed.

"We've tried, so many times. There's nothing we can do." He hung his head in shameful defeat, waiting for his judgment. Heavy drops of water fell silently until crashing into the leaf litter. I guessed we shared the custom of crying.

It hadn't been my sister. It had been someone who had hidden from the evacuation, but my sister was in this hell too. How was I going to protect her? The man in front of me was the strongest person I'd ever seen, and a bunch of them couldn't stop that creature from ripping away one of the few precious lives sent to help them. I realized that's why there weren't enough women here. They'd been hunted, and it wasn't going to stop.

I suddenly had to sit. My nervous energy couldn't keep me on my feet any longer. I was in shock.

Chapter Five
Safety

Drex

The woman was falling from her feet, and even as I helped her to the ground, she had fainted. In my arms, she was terrifyingly small. Her bosom rose and fell to show she was still breathing. I pulled my eyes away from the tantalizing curve of her breasts evident through her suit. I patted her face in an attempt to rouse her. Her skin was soft under my hands too calloused to be a prince's hands. Just like the humans who had come before her, she had no horns, and no knots, except for the center one for her nose. She murmured a bit, her eyelids fluttered, but she was still limp in my arms. We didn't have time for her to recover. I needed to get her to safety.

Most of the Xavians had already rushed the other humans to safety, scattering like we had learned to do. I scooped her up easily. She felt cool against my chest, and the heat from my body escaped me and funneled into her. This would be an advantage to her and her species—it's believed the Orkain used thermal sensory to hunt us. Our females have a much warmer body temperature than our men. I kept her close as I moved swiftly through the jungle to my home.

I didn't even know her name.

I did know that I'd almost staggered when I saw her emerge from the spaceship. Her soft body, smooth skin, and curve of her hips had made me forget about the menace flying above us for a moment. It had been a dangerous reaction. I stomped through the thick vegetation, not caring to avoid sticky vines. I had been an idiot. I had let too many of us gather, and I had shown everyone that the Earth women's arrival wasn't going to change anything. They'd be killed just as easily.

We had only gotten halfway to my house, before she roused and began fighting against my carry, twisting her body against mine for leverage. Her small arms and hands pulled at my own around her. She couldn't remove them, but I was relieved that she seemed to be recovering so quickly. Her moxie wasn't a surprise at this point—rather than running for cover, she'd stayed and directed her people off of the ship. And when one of them had been picked up by a monster three times her size, she'd run directly at it. She was brave for her size.

"It's OK. I'm going to set you down," I jumbled through what I hoped were reassuring words to her.

I kept my hands on her torso to be sure she was steady on her feet before I let go. She yanked her body away.

"Where are you taking me? Where is my sister?" Her eyes searched the dense jungle, and widened as she realized she was alone with me. Even in the shadows, I could see her eyes were different than ours. The dark center was small, and the ring of color much larger—

hers with piercing greens and browns like summer milcress.

I gave her distance and showed her my palms in surrender. I wasn't going to hurt her. Lowree had told me these women had been dropped here under pretense. I explained, "We were attacked by the Orkain. Procedure is to scatter and take shelter. I'm taking you to safety."

"Oh, like hell you are," she said. She took a defensive stance and began searching the ground around her, maybe for some sort of weapon. "Take me back to the ship. Take me back to my sister."

"Your people aren't back at the ship. Your sister is with another Xavian."

"Why have you separated us?!"

"The Orkain see body heat. We can't—we shouldn't have—gathered in such large numbers. We're split up to keep us safe. You fainted. I'm just trying to get you somewhere safe. Your sister? Which one was she?" I desperately tried to get her on my side.

"She helped me and Sophie move the women out. She was one of the last on the ramp with me. Sophie had dark hair. My sister, Sara, she has brown hair like me." She held up a handful of her hair that had debris in it, but looked quite silky otherwise.

"She went with Vance, my adviser. She will be safe with him." I was thankful to have an answer for her. Vance had stayed and helped until the last minute. He had even attacked the Orkain with me.

Her stance became less defensive as her panic seemed to lessen. "Your adviser?"

I took the opportunity. "My name is Drex. I'm Prince of the Xavians—at least, what is left of them."

I extended my hand in the way that the human government had taught me.

She shook my hand warily. "I'm Katy. You're a prince?" My cheeks warmed in the attention her eyes gave me, even as they cut at me skeptically. I gave a sheepish grin in reply.

"Kay-tee," I tried. My tongues tripped over themselves. She tossed a weak smile in my direction at my attempt, and I felt my heart jolt against my ribcage. "I am devastated to hear that you've been brought here under pretense. I promise no harm will come to you or your people—" even as I said it, the words cut like knives in my gut, "—by my people," I was forced to add. With a deep breath, I continued, "Please let me take you somewhere safe. More Orkain could be coming."

Katy kept her distance from me, but she allowed me to escort her to my home. I was thankful for it, but what other choice did she have? She'd been abandoned by her government. They hadn't even escorted them onto the planet and introduced them properly. I hoped the Earth women weren't as treacherous as their mankind.

It hadn't been a proper matching, but I assumed Katy would be staying with me, and her sister with Vance. I had lucked out. If I were to be with any of the other hosts for an extended period of time, I was glad it would be with Vance, and not with some random subject of mine. I was still quite unsure and nervous, and I didn't want to have to present an image of princely confidence to one of my men while trying to navigate interactions with Katy.

Katy was absolutely beautiful, but with the dishonesty that had brought her here, I didn't expect anything to actually happen between us. I was actually kind of thankful. I didn't want to be forced into a relationship any more than I assumed she did. Scooping up a woman who arrived under pretense wasn't the start of a romantic story at all. It was nothing like rotha. First, she was a different species. While I was sure they had zarata—the awareness that set us apart from beasts, I wasn't sure if they experienced rotha as an actual biological change as we did. Lowree and her beloved had matching spots on their skin, so had my parents.

I felt obligated as prince to find a mate, despite clinging to the romantic notions of rotha. I didn't want to mate out of obligation or to simply further the species. Like I said, I would have rather been a prince in more prosperous times when my abilities and decisions wouldn't have mattered much.

I couldn't come up with a way to communicate to Katy that she was more than safe at my house—that I hadn't been anxiously awaiting the arrival of a womb to bear my children—without sounding pompous. And why would she believe me anyway? I was already failing at the most basic things—keeping her and her people safe. I kept quiet and hoped my insufficiencies were done showing their heads to my guest for the evening.

Chapter Six
His Home

Katy

Partially in shock, I followed him. I didn't want to be wherever in the jungle we were anymore. That woman getting abducted was terrifying. I didn't want to be here when the beast came back.

This wasn't what I signed up for. Obviously. No wonder the government had lied to us. There's no way I'd have agreed or let my sister agree to being sent as a fertile womb to further the genetic lines of an alien species, especially on a planet that seemed to be ruled by large, devilish predators.

And it got worse. I hadn't quite processed it when I had exited the ship—seeing as there were monsters flying overhead—but it hadn't been a ship at all. What we had woken up in, was all that there was. It must have been separated from the ship and just dropped off, like a pod. I thought to look up at the sky, now that we were on a cleared path. Perhaps it was still in orbit, watching us.

"Is the ship still around?" I asked.

"It's gone. We thought it strange."

I nodded, but still kept glancing at the sky. I didn't necessarily trust his answer. He had reason to lie to me. It was better if I thought I was stuck here.

The path got exceedingly smaller, then I was led to the bottom of a hill, where I realized we had walked atop an underground house. There was an overhang of earth as a covered patio, and a door that led into the hill, itself. He opened the door, and the lights came on automatically. He gestured for me to go inside.

"Whoa, is this your private house? Are you serious? Take me to the others." I hadn't even thought that he'd be absconding me to his personal home. What a creep!

"I'm so sorry. I didn't think to explain. We don't have a place to gather like that. The Orkain, remember? Yes, this is my home, but please come inside and be safe while we figure everything out."

"I need to see my sister."

"We can do that," he said, brightening. "We can video call her, and the others, make sure they are all right. Please." He gestured inside again.

I stepped in reluctantly.

It didn't look much different from a typical house on Earth; although, I didn't know what half of the stuff was. With all the surrounding jungle, I had assumed they were more primitive. Still, it didn't look how I imagined a prince's house would look like, if he was a prince at all.

"I apologize my house isn't very technologically advanced. We've had to change everything when those creatures arrived. A lot of houses had to be built at once and they don't have a lot of the luxuries that we are used to."

A pit started in my stomach. Did I really look that judgmental, that he knew what I was thinking?

"The Orkain are new?"

"They arrived a generation ago. They have infrared vision. They seek heat. That's why we've moved underground and separate from each other."

The entry opened to what I suspected was a living space or parlor to entertain guests. There was a soft-looking leather extended couch—the Xavians were larger than humans—and a low coffee table. The decorations were sparse. There weren't a lot of personal touches; no photos of his family or the family dog. Did they have dogs on this planet? There was a typical hallway with maybe three or four doors off of it. Two rooms came off of the living space, a kitchen with a table, and an office-looking space with a desk and a mirror larger than the full-length ones of Earth.

I wasn't about to explore the rest of the house. I didn't want him to get any ideas. And, I wanted to be near the exit. He offered me a seat on the couch, and I took the very far end to maintain distance.

He asked, "Is it true that your government didn't tell you this was a reproductive program?" It appeared to be a question he'd been wanting to ask for a while.

The term 'reproductive program' made my stomach churn.

"We had no idea."

"Fryyre," came that curse word again. "I want you to know. You have my personal word that no one is going to participate in any reproductive program without their consent. I can't believe it."

His word didn't mean much to me, but at least he considered lying to me about it. I was worried that their society was even worse than my own, that he wouldn't even recognize our rights.

"Did you like…buy us?" I asked. My face scrunched up in pain and disgust.

"No, not at all. Fryyre. We were told that you all were knowledgeable in the whole thing, that your world saw the benefits of keeping this world due to the holmium content in it, and that by participating in extending our genetic line, we'd be able to set up a hybrid type colony here and all benefit. I was firm that no one would be required to copulate. This was an opportunity for your female kind to visit and decide if you wanted to make a life here. I was skeptical that anyone would want to take that sort of risk. I guess your government was, too."

"So do you think they still plan to come back a year from now?" I shuddered, refusing to explore the answer in either direction.

"I would think so. They haven't gotten the holmium, yet. When they come, we will set this all straight."

I nodded, but I didn't believe him. No matter how respectful he talked or how surprised he looked, he had still participated in this female-trafficking and reproduction scheme. Nothing about this was OK. My entire government had tricked me, and this guy was lying to me, too.

"Why do you move your head like that?"

I had to think for a moment about what he was talking about. "Oh, it's what we call a 'nod.' A nod means 'yes' or 'I agree' and if you shake your head, that's a 'no.'" I demonstrated what I meant.

His head jerked up and down as he tried out the nod.

I smiled. "You said I could speak with my sister?"

He nodded, a little less drastically this time, and led me to the office-like room. The walls were a soft plum color. There was a massive desk with a chair behind it, and less comfortable seating in front of it for guests. I guessed he did his princely duties here, whatever they were. The oversized mirror turned out to be some sort of communication device that he called a settit. He voiced a command to it in his language and its screen woke up, which was taller than Drex by several inches. He gave it another command and while I didn't understand the interface, it was clearly a standby screen while it connected.

"What's your language called?"

"Xavian, same as our people."

A life-size Xavian appeared on the screen. He was a lighter green than Drex, almost a robin's egg blue. I remembered him vaguely from our earlier interaction. His horns were dark, wrapped with black stripes. He was just as good-looking as Drex with strong limbs and thick muscles. His eyes shone brightly through the screen. Behind his mass though, peeked my sister. When she saw it was me, she leaped from behind him.

"Oh my gosh!" she shouted, then jumped up and down.

"Are you OK?" I asked, rushing closer to the screen. She didn't seem to be harmed bodily. She almost looked happy.

"Yes! Vance saved me. You've got one too!"

Vance's shoulders came up in some sort of shrug. From the expression on his face, I read some embarrassment.

"Are you sure you're OK?" I searched her face and body again to convince myself. It took me a moment to realize she had said, 'You've got one, too.' "Uh yes,

Drex has taken me to his home for now. I'd love to be with you, though."

Drex shook his head just off-camera. He was apparently already understanding the usefulness of such silent gestures.

"Can I go see her?" I asked Drex, hoping the answer would be different, out loud and in their presence.

"No, it's best we stay inside for a while."

Sara shrugged and cut her eyes to Vance and gave me a sly smile. Clearly, she was enjoying Vance's company. The government probably hadn't even needed to lie to Sara. She would've been on board with alien sex. I hoped to God, she wouldn't.

"Please, please be safe, Sara."

"Of course! I'm safe here with Vance," she said as if he wasn't an alien that had just brought her to his lair after another alien attacked them. For all they knew, the Orkain were saving them from the Xavian. I couldn't imagine that really, but the dude was a stranger. Sara had little self-preservation skills… that was why I was here.

Sara and I said goodbye. Drex and Vance shared a few words in their language and then the screen disconnected.

"I told him that if he did anything disrespectful, I would tear his head off," he said, reassuring me.

"Uh, thanks, that's…nice." It was difficult to tell if he was making a joke or if he was serious. Either way, I guess it was good for Sara.

The mirror thing started making noise and swirling with color.

"I have to take this call. Are you OK?" he asked.

"A prince gotta prince," I said.

He looked at me, confused, but didn't ask about it. I motioned that I'd be in the other room, and took my leave.

I didn't know what to think about my interaction with my sister. Something wasn't right. What difference would it make for one more person to be here, or for me to be there? Vance could live with Drex for all I cared. And hadn't the creature already…eaten? I shuddered with the thought. I wasn't about to bring it up; that was probably a bit crude and inconsiderate. Still, how often did the Orkain need to eat? Or whatever it was they were doing with them?

Drex might have been telling the truth about the Orkain about sensing temperature. Their females were a lot warmer. I had felt it when they came aboard. Human women were even cooler than the Xavian males, and were smaller than both genders. So we were actually the least likely to be seen by the Orkain. I wondered if they were separating us to keep us confused and unable to make decisions as a group. Divide and conquer, wasn't that a technique for…something? I didn't know. It was hard to even think after all that had happened. Maybe I was still in shock, but I did know I needed to find my sister. I slipped out the door and quietly shut it behind me.

I wasn't immediately exposed, as the patio was covered. I searched the sky and into the trees—I didn't know if they landed in them, or what I'd do if I saw that half-human, half-demon beast sitting on a tree branch staring at me. I didn't know anything. This was stupid.

I didn't see anything scary. In fact, it was pretty. The sky was a crisp blue like in autumn, but still hot and steamy like a summer day. I hope our government had thought to give us plenty of sunscreen. Eventually, we'd have to go back to the ship to gather what supplies we had been given. Perhaps we could all stay in the ship. It seemed just as safe as Drex's house—at least if we could get the door shut—and we'd all have our own space and could be together.

Stepping out from the covering was scary. I couldn't help but crouch as I crept to the tree line. It was like an instinct. My body refused to straighten, like it was ready to dive to the ground at a moment's notice. I tried to stay out of sight of the hill's exterior windows, and followed the tree line back the way we had come. I had seen a few trails into the woods, and I was hoping that my sister was in a hill-hut somewhere not too far. If I found any of the other women, I'd try to recruit them too, if just so we can all have a discussion together. We had all been pulled apart so quickly without knowing what was going on. I didn't want the wool pulled over our eyes again.

I reached a fork in the path, and I couldn't quite remember which one we had taken. The foliage surrounding both was so thick. The leaves of some of the plants were bigger than my face. The shorter plants were as tall as me. There was little to see in either direction. I looked at the path and how it forked. One of the paths was wider and had seen more use than the other. Assuming that we had taken the more used path to his house, and that a smaller path would be to someone else's house, I chose the path less traveled.

I was feeling pretty good about how I'd come to my decision. I was in no way a nature-girl. All the flowers and branches and stuff I was involved with had come at premium prices and had been expertly manicured and placed expensively on tables, archways, and along aisles, so I was pretty impressed that I had even thought of it. However, in just thirty or so yards, the trail seemed to have disappeared, and I was left looking at just a dense jungle. Was it a dead end?

Then I remembered that Drex's home had been facing the opposite way of his path in. You could only see the roof of it and that was hidden underground. I could indeed be close to someone's home, but just not be able to see it at the moment. I tried to study the ground, but I couldn't make heads or tails of it. So much for my innate tracking skills. I looked to see if there was any way to go to lower ground where a door might be seen. I saw nothing, and I was afraid to wander too far from the end of the path. There was a chance I would lose it and then I'd be screwed.

I chalked this one up to a loss and turned back around. I would try another path and see if I could find another hut. Maybe I'd learn some patterns or something. It was harder to backtrack than I anticipated. Clouds rolled in and gave everything a weird hue. Alien planet. What was I thinking?

I should have reached that intersection by now. It hadn't been far from that fork before I'd reached the dead-end, right? I wondered if I should turn around and backtrack again. I wasn't even sure if I was currently on a path. I looked both ways and couldn't distinguish a path in either direction. The clouds rolled thicker overhead, and the jungle darkened. The rosy hue of the sky made me feel unsteady. And I wondered how much sunlight there would be left today. I hadn't gone that far from Drex's place…at least, I didn't think I did. Gosh, I was getting lost.

OK, honestly, I was already totally lost.

No doubt about it.

There was little hope of getting my bearings back, but perhaps I could find another trail. Then at least I could follow it from one end to the other and maybe find some help. Or, if anything, sit and wait to be 'rescued' by my captors/traffickers. Ugh. I hated feeling helpless. I took a deep breath, in and out. And I tried to look around for some sign—close or distant—of a clearing or a trail or…something.

And then I heard them. The jungle had been relatively quiet, which made the noise that much scarier.

It was the flapping of wings.

I instinctively looked overhead but didn't see anything…yet.

My body wanted to bolt, to just take off. I pleaded with it not to. I found the biggest tree to take cover under. As much as I wanted to charge to the tree, I took one step at a time, slowly, to try not to disturb anything, to not make too much noise. Then when I reached the tree, I sat down and wrapped my arms and legs around it. That beast was going to have to wrench me from this tree. I held on tight.

The beating of wings got louder, then quieter, then louder, like it was zipping around nearby. I hope it hadn't already had its eyes set on me and was now just playing with its prey. My heart thumped so loudly. It felt like it was smashing against the tree. My body shook. I wondered if it was making the entire tree tremble, like a vibrating signal to the beast that wanted to take me up into the sky and…devour me? Drex had said they were hunting, but I guess I didn't know what that meant. Was it for food? For sport? Did they also need females?

OK, I was terrified. My thoughts were scattered everywhere.

A wind I hadn't felt before accompanied the sound of the wings. It was close. I gulped loudly and tried silently to convince my body to drop a few degrees. Think cold thoughts, I thought. It didn't make any sense. Fear had made me do crazy things, like run out into this terror.

The beast was looking for me. It hadn't found me yet, but it was gradually circling in. It flew close to the ground, disturbing the foliage, darting around. I urged myself not to move, but my head continued to keep it in sight. Its legs moved erratically, seemingly for no reason but perhaps they had some sort of sensing power, like whiskers on them or for smell. They were creepy. More than once I caught sight of its horned crown. It was definitely closing on me. And all I could do was clutch my tree. Even if I could get my body to move (it was now refusing), I would not be able to outrun that creature.

I thought of my little sister. How I had thoroughly screwed this up and had been absolutely no use to her. I hadn't even found her. I was just going to be gone, never to be seen again. And Sara was going to have to navigate this world all by herself. Tears started sliding down my face.

Suddenly, the beast screeched a massive wail. My body which had refused to move, did, as my hands covered my ears to protect them. The sound reverberated and burned inside my skull. The creature had found me for sure, but when I opened my eyes, I realized it had found someone else.

The Orkain landed in silent, graceful terror. It kept its wing at full extension even as its wide, hocked claws splayed on the ground. It landed right in front of Drex, who stood staunch still, staring it down. I screamed, but Drex did not flinch. And, if the beast could hear me, it did not bother with me either. Its arms and hands, disgustingly similar to a human's reached out and felt for Drex. Could they not see at all?

I watched in disgust as it touched Drex's face and shoulders and chest. I hardly knew Drex but I felt protective of him. And these motions were clearly unwanted, a violation. Anger boiled inside me—all the anger at the unfairness of the situation I'd been put in, and the situation I was watching now. The beast finished feeling him, let out a blood-curdling scream, and shot off through the gap in the green canopy it had created with its downward rush.

The stoic man dropped to his knees. "Katye? Katye?" he called; his voice thick.

I thought about sitting there and not answering. I thought about staying hidden. I didn't know if he was a threat, but there were obviously true dangers out here. He'd just survived one.

I went to say, "I'm here," but it came out like a small croak. My mouth and throat weren't working. My whole body felt terror.

Still, the noise seemed thankfully to be enough. He turned in my direction. I tried to wave, but my arms and legs were clutching the tree again and would not, did not, let go.

The sheer panic in his eyes softened when he caught sight of me. He jumped up and raced over to me. His thick long legs bounded and closed the distance so quickly. He put his strong arms over my arms, his face close to mine.

"It's OK. You're safe now," he said. He gently pulled my arms off the tree, and he embraced me as my legs relaxed. Hugging me from behind, I felt some sense of safety and relief that I hadn't felt since well, way before any of this space stuff happened. But maybe even before then.

I couldn't help it. I trembled in his arms. His chest and body were much larger than mine, and I felt enveloped but not in a bad or scary way. He was right. I felt safe. I felt safe now. His cheek was against the side of my face, and I could feel his hot breath in my ear and on my cheek. Despite his purposefully slow breathing, he still breathed heavily. He had been looking for me; he had been concerned for me. Suddenly I felt sort of bad for running off. Of course, I cared for my sister, but maybe this had been a dumb thing to do. I mean, of course, it was dumb. And I'd made someone feel the same way I felt for my sister—scared and worried. We hardly knew each other, but I didn't want anyone to feel that sort of panic.

"How did you know that would work?" The beast had examined him and left.

"I didn't," he said simply, but his voice gave away his fear.

The Orkain had been searching for me. He basically sacrificed himself, hoping he'd be taken instead of me? I trembled in wonder at the thought. Why would he do that for me?

"It's getting dark. May I take you home?" he asked.

He didn't scold me for leaving. He didn't demand I return to his home. He was asking if that's what I would like to do. And yeah, I was ready to go back to his home.

I nodded, and he helped pick me up from the ground. He moved around to the front of me and looked me over, worryingly. His brows pressed together and the center of his eyes specked green. I could tell he was asking permission for something. I nodded again, and he began pulling some debris off of my clothes, gently swiping things off. I felt like a child who couldn't take care of themselves. And maybe I couldn't in this world.

I was still shaking so he kept an arm around me while he led me through the woods. I didn't mind. I was impressed that he seemed to know exactly where we were going. Pride was a silly thing, but part of me secretly hoped I had wandered far from the path before becoming lost.

It did take several minutes to find anything path-like, and even longer to reach a wide, frequently used path, possibly the one that led to the path to his house. Besides being saved the embarrassment of being lost just steps from a path, I realized he had gone pretty far into the jungle to find me. I had apparently been sort of trouble, but he wasn't acting like it. He seemed thankful to have found me, mostly unscathed.

Darkness had taken over, and I didn't even notice our switch to the smaller path or our arrival atop his home again. We walked around to the entrance. He opened the door for me. The lights turned on again automatically, but the windows remained dark from the outside. I assumed it also kept the heat from escaping the home. I was thankful to go inside.

"May I show you your room?" he asked.

I found my voice. I hadn't attempted to say anything since the woods. "My own room?"

"Yes…I'm sorry if I didn't explain earlier that you'll have private space here." He then hesitated. "Is that why you ran off? I'm so sorry."

And he did seem very apologetic, more apologetic than he should for it being me that ran away. He hadn't done anything wrong, but he seemed to think he had.

"No, but um, thank you. Yes, I'd love to see it."

He led me down the hallway and gave me the remainder of the tour that had been interrupted by the call. The first room was a bathroom, from what I gathered. I wasn't quite sure about the functions of all the devices. I would need another tour of that stuff, I guessed.

"Your room is here," he pointed to the door. "And mine is across the hall."

He opened the door to my room and gestured for me to go in on my own. He gave a small bow and walked back to the living area, as a nice way to give me a chance to clean up, or at least regroup, without him staring me down the entire time. I was thankful for it.

I closed the door and was grateful to see some sort of locking mechanism. I wondered if he'd had that installed for me, to make me feel safer. It worked. I felt safer. I locked it quietly and then looked around the rest of the room. It was strangely familiar.

While the other furniture in the house had been alien, this stuff was clearly made by looking at photos of furniture from Earth. They'd done their best to make a room that would feel familiar to their guests. At least, they tried. There was the biggest bed I had ever seen. It was longer and wider than a California King…which was already a bed much too big for my small frame. Next to the bed was a vanity and a chest of drawers, which seemed to be actually the correct size. I opened the drawers and was surprised to see clothes inside. They had tried to think of everything. It was clear they had put some thought into this and hadn't just thought they were buying females for sex. I felt a bit bad for the things I had thought about them. Given the way females had been treated in our history, it'd been an understandable assumption. We'd been dropped off here with just a video. The cowards.

I pulled out the clothes to find they were all different sizes. That made me feel even better, that they weren't expecting a certain body type to arrive. I guess they hadn't put in any type of request of what we would look like. Although, our government had definitely sent them young—and now I assumed our fertility had been verified—fertile females. I found what would be a loose-fitting tunic and some equally soft linen pants. I took off my tight-fitting 'space suit' and it felt good to put on these soft, flowing fabrics. I checked the stitching. It was nice and durable, and clearly hand sewn. That made the clothes feel even more special. I would have to sort out what would fit and then pass on what wouldn't…wait, was I thinking about staying here?

Well, *here* was the operative word. I was pretty sure I was going to have to stay on this planet. I didn't have a spaceship. And I got the impression that the Xavians didn't have a spaceship either. We'd see if Earth showed up anytime soon…ugh, I didn't want to think about them never coming back. That was just too much to swallow at this point. They would come back for the holmium, right? I hoped they wouldn't find an easier source before it was time to come fetch us. But yeah, maybe I could stay here. I needed to see my sister, but clearly, I was going to have to rely on Drex for that.

I checked myself in the mirror and was shocked to see the face staring back at me. I had forgotten that I had aged a few months in that stasis chamber…*stasis, my ass*…I hadn't yet gotten used to my appearance. I wondered if it had only been three months, or if they'd lied about that too. I finger combed the leaf debris from my hair. My state surprised me because Drex had been looking at me so…I don't know, like I was desirable? Definitely not like I had a bunch of dirt in my hair.

I looked inside the vanity and found a fork.

A fork?

That Disney version of *The Little Mermaid* came into my mind, as I imagined brushing my hair with the fork. I wonder where exactly they'd gotten their information for humans. It was close, but obviously, they had to make some decisions without human guidance.

I didn't brush my hair with the fork.

I pulled out all the leaves I could see and feel. I wiped the dried dirt from my arms. I had cleaned up well on the ship, and despite that being two scary encounters since, I didn't look completely awful. At least, I looked OK enough to reemerge from the bedroom. I didn't want him to worry I had run away again.

I quietly unlocked the door, opened it, and tiptoed out. The light in the room he called his was off, so I went down the hallway to the living space. I found him in his office, with his back to me, talking on the settit.

They were speaking in their native language and so I couldn't understand what they were saying. The man on the screen wasn't Sara's alien. It was another. He had the same shades of turquoise that Drex had, but his eyes sparkled violet which was complimentary. His thick horns grew somewhat sideways and towards each other forming giant brows from a distance. He wore several layers of tight leather. I got the feeling it wasn't practical outside in the midday heat, but was something he was wearing for some sort of event, maybe this call.

The alien that was on the screen spotted me in the hallway and motioned to Drex to tell him he was no longer alone. Drex looked over to me in surprise, then gave me a little bow of apology.

I shook my head to let him know it wasn't necessary, although I think that caused more confusion than I intended since he just knew it as '*no.*'

"I'm sorry. Please continue your conversation. I can go back into my room for a little bit."

"No, no," he said, waving me closer to the screen and out from the shadows of the hallway. "This concerns you; you can be here. Please meet Davian, he is um, a…communications officer for our people." He struggled to find the right title in English. "He is calling all of the host homes and checking to make sure everyone is OK."

Davian the Xavian, I rhymed in my head.

"Yes, I'd like to know how you are doing. Drex knows better than to be standing here while I ask, even if he is the prince."

So, he was a prince.

Drex took his leave and moved to the kitchen.

"Now, I have great respect for Drex from a professional standpoint, but I have never interacted with him as a female, alone, in his own home, so I am asking with great seriousness. Please answer silently with nods or head shakes, as Lanie taught me."

I nodded.

I realized how ubiquitous our head gestures were that someone else had also naturally taught it in the few hours we had been here. Actually, I didn't know how to reference time here. How long were days? How did they tell time? I was becoming kind of curious about the planet. I had so many questions for Drex.

"Have you been asked to do anything you haven't wanted to do?"

That was an interesting question. I had just run away. I'm sure Drex had told him that, or…maybe he hadn't. Sort of embarrassing for both of us. But in truth, he hadn't asked me to do anything.

I shook my head.

"You do not have to stay with this man. Do you want someone to retrieve you?"

I was just learning to trust Drex. There was no way I wanted to start over with someone else. Not tonight.

"I want to know about my people. You said you've talked to Sophie. How is she? And my sister, I want to see her. Her name is Sara."

It was Davian's turn to nod his head.

"Sophie was in general a bit umm… combative, but she said she would like to stay at least the night at her host's house. We may need to switch her to another's which would best be done earlier so that everyone can begin to get accustomed without major changes involved. Sara was enthusiastic and said she was having a great time—"

I shook my head with a smile.

"I'm sorry you don't believe me? What is going on?"

I laughed. "I guess head gestures are a bit more complex than we give them credit. I was merely gesturing a sort of… sarcasm? I don't even know how to describe it. It was a gesture of knowing that she'd have a unique experience here from the rest of us."

"Ah, I understand. I think."

He told me about the nine other women to whom he'd already spoken, and it sounded all right. I hadn't gotten everyone's names. I had thought there would be plenty of time for that.

"Are there any more questions you have for me?" he asked. He had a big congenial smile which made me feel more at ease, even given the situation. I wasn't sure if they aged the same as we did, but he seemed to be a bit older than Drex. I couldn't quite place it. Maybe it was the beaten horns. I didn't at the moment, and I found I actually preferred to ask Drex.

"You can come in!" I said a bit louder towards the kitchen. A few moments later, Drex reappeared.

"Did I pass the test?" he asked. I thought it was a joke but he had worry written on his face, less intense than when he talked about the Orkain but not far from it. I guess maybe he thought that my running away was an expression of how I felt about him and his home. I felt a bit bad for that, but at the same time, felt it was a perfectly acceptable reaction to being trafficked.

"You did," Davian said, "for now."

Drex smiled, but it didn't quite relieve all the worry on his face.

"Are you sure you want to stay with me?" he asked.

"I've got nowhere better to be at the moment," I joked. "But I do want to see my sister."

"I see that," he said with a side smile. Then he turned to Davian. "Did you tell her how the others are faring?"

"I did. And that we might have to switch Sophie's and Tessa's host homes. They're the two that seem to be having some minor personality clashes, but they both assured me that they felt safe for tonight. I'll reach out again to them in the morning."

"Okay, please have someone stop by their houses tonight as patrol. I want to know if there seems to be any commotion, or any trouble that we're not able to pick up on from a video call."

Davian nodded dutifully. "Understood. We have to be understanding of the trauma they've gone through. It's not our fault, but we absolutely have to take care now. We cannot make it worse for them. I mean…I just don't know how they're going to learn to trust us coming from a society where they couldn't trust their own people. We're complete strangers."

I was glad that Drex didn't seem to be the only one with some sense around here. Maybe this place wouldn't be too bad to hold up in, at least until our people came back to get us.

Chapter Seven
Sweet

Drex

I had taken a risk by not telling Davian that Katy had run away. I'd told myself it was to maintain her privacy—that she should be able to decide what was said to whom—but I was also embarrassed. I had an image to maintain. I'd been a dunce allowing her to run off into danger. If I can't keep a woman safe for half an hour, how am I supposed to care for my people? As prince, I couldn't very well be the first to lose hosting privileges. So, I'd stayed quiet.

While she was being interviewed by Davian, I'd busied myself in the kitchen, preparing her some food. I didn't know how stasis worked, but she had to be hungry by now. I didn't know what she would like to eat, so I readied a bunch of stuff for her to try.

She hadn't been here a day, and she was already a pain in my life. Headstrong. Stupid. Still, I was a little impressed. She had been a brave woman to do that. I thought she'd be satisfied enough to see her sister through the communicator, but obviously not. I hadn't expected her to run off. I had my reasons for telling her '*no.*' Now she'd seen those reasons twice, and still, I wasn't sure if she cared at all. As fiery as she was, I couldn't imagine her being tricked by her government like she'd been. I imagined her sister had created that weak spot in her logic.

The annoyance was new though. When I realized she'd gone missing, I had only been terrified. I immediately went searching for her. She wasn't at Vance's home where Sara was; although, I assumed that was where she had intended to go despite not knowing anything about anywhere or how to get there. I'd asked Vance to keep a look out for her, but to keep it secret. It was sort of embarrassing that I'd lost my woman, right? As much as I respected her for being her own person, she also was on an unknown planet, and it was just dumb to go wandering around. I should have stopped it. She could've died out there, picked up by that Orkain. Vance promised he would be quiet about his watch. He decided not to tell Sara at the time; he didn't want to worry her. Also, we both assumed she'd escape to look for her sister. We had to assume that brave dumbness ran in the family.

As I made my way from Vance's place, I found a few places from where I might be able to track her. They were places that someone had walked a few times, maybe her...I wasn't the best tracker. I was in government. Our hunters were trackers. Maybe I should have recruited one of them, but I hadn't the time. It was getting dark, and I wanted to see if I could find her first before raising all the alarms, which I would absolutely do if darkness fell. Then I saw the Orkain. It was a medium-sized one, perhaps had come back from a long hunt and had just heard about our gathering...if they communicated at all... because he was sort of late. I followed the Orkain because unfortunately, I worried that he might be a better tracker than myself. The sun was setting, and I knew the ground would be cooling, making it even easier for the Orkain to spot Katy.

When it started hovering in one area, my heart quickened. Had it found what I could not? I struggled with wanting to stay out of its sights and wanting to be close to anything it was near. If I was out of range, then it could get to her before I could. It would mean I was also out of range to save Katy. It wailed, and I knew it was honing in on her. Not knowing where she was, I jumped out in front of the beast. I hadn't the time to think. If I did, I guessed I would've realized I was sacrificing myself. However, it caught the Orkain off guard. It stopped…realized I wasn't a woman and flew off. I felt a combination of relief and sickness; I was thankful to still be alive but repulsed by the invasion I experienced. Hearing Katy's whimper, and finding her safe, helped me put it aside for a moment.

She'd wrapped herself around a large tree. It was smart. The tree had warmth from the sun, and she had conformed to its shape. Still, despite being smart, she was still entirely out of her depth. So was I if I intended to keep her safe. Her small body trembling in my arms kept my own from trembling.

My thoughts were interrupted by Katy calling me out of the kitchen and back to the office. I re-entered, and the phone call with Davian ended shortly thereafter. Then we fell into some awkwardness. It was clear she hadn't told Davian about her excursion. I considered thanking her for not making me look like an idiot. I also considered thanking her for not having run away again in the last ten minutes.

"I don't want to stay on this planet," she interjected the silence and my thoughts.

Her statement surprised me. Did she think I had a way to get her off this planet? I didn't. If my people were capable of space flight, I'd take them somewhere else, like Earth. Although, it didn't sound all that safe there. Our females would be second-class citizens, or worse. We didn't abide with that here. If anything, women had become more revered with our societal changes. No matter, I couldn't blame Katy for not trusting…anyone. Her government, supposed to protect and serve her, had lied to her. And I wasn't even that. I was a stranger.

"I wish I had a way to get you home. I'm sorry." I said, and I was honest about that. It didn't help us for her to have been lied to. None of this was going to work without her permission, her enthusiasm, her help. I didn't see how any of this could work anyway. I was sorry about all of it. Earth would benefit from our relationship and our continued existence as a species. Our planet was rich with resources we didn't necessarily need at the moment (and we had the means to mine it, easily). Their planet was rich with resources too…of a different sort. I couldn't even fathom the number when they told me how many people were on Earth.

Katy probably thought the worst of me for agreeing to accept Earth women for holmium. It wasn't like that though. We weren't purchasing "willing females" or "wombs." We were just looking for a program to bring women who may be those things to be introduced to us. These were supposed to be women aware of the opportunities and the *possibility* of procreation. These women dropped off couldn't have consented because they didn't know the truth. And this was far beyond the consent of a potential singular sexual act. They had their own people, families, culture. They had their own lives. They were promised cultural exchange, not maybe losing everything they'd ever known. I couldn't express those thoughts, though. I had to be optimistic. I'd been wondering if they'd chosen women that didn't have a lot of ties to their Earth… it was both deceptive and effective. It wouldn't surprise me. Either way, these women didn't know they were being dropped off here to possibly stay forever. And, they hadn't told them about the Orkain. About how the Orkain had wiped out huge numbers of us before we even understood anything about them. We did everything wrong. We huddled in masses for safety, so we could fight. Now we know that just made it easier for them to find us. And our weapons? They were impervious to all of them. We still haven't recorded a definitive death of one of those things caused directly by us. Between the Orkain and the deceptive humans, I was beginning to wonder if the universe had any decent, upright beings.

I didn't know what to say to her concerning the fairness of the galaxy, so I asked if she was hungry. This was apparently the one right thing I had done all day.

She nodded vigorously, and I motioned for her to follow me into the kitchen, where I had a small table. I pulled out the chair so she could sit; she seemed surprised by the action. It was still unusual for me to see two chairs at the table (although I had four around here for it). I had set her chair there the other day, not knowing what things would be like. I couldn't have imagined it would be like this at all.

I didn't have any preconceived beliefs that my rotha was going to be arriving on the ship from Earth. It wasn't that I didn't believe in rotha. It had existed for generations before me, and for my parents, which meant I was here because of it, but Xavia had changed a great, incredible deal since then. Our population had been decimated. To think that there were destined pairs in what was left, in these ruins…it was an impractical belief to carry. Rotha had been effectively killed by the Orkain. Personally, I would never find it. However, I couldn't express that opinion as the leader of Xavia. It would throw away generations of tradition. So I've been careful not to say a word against the ways that led us here, even if they no longer make sense.

She was, of course, incredibly beautiful, but I wasn't holding any realistic expectations that something would work out between us. However, I had at least expected that the woman who stayed with me would actually want to be on this planet. Fryyre, I just needed to keep the peace. She wasn't here for love, and neither was I. However, I couldn't give her what she really wanted—which was to return to Earth with her sister. And who could blame her? But the thing was, she didn't have a way back home, and I didn't have a way for her, either. The ship, as I understood it, had left. It would probably be back, eventually, for the holmium, because I imagine they didn't just drop us off this 'gift' of women. They'd want something in return, but for now—she was stuck on this planet. And if that was the case, it was important that she remain with me. I needed to keep up appearances. If I couldn't keep a woman in my house, how was I supposed to convince anyone else this was going to work? I had worked that part in my head over and over before the ship had even arrived. No one—neither my people nor humans—would have faith if I didn't appear to have faith. The Xavian Prince had to participate and appear successful at least for a time. I needed her.

I set the plate of various foods in front of Katy.

"I wasn't sure what you'd like, so I brought you several things to try."

She eyed them nervously. "What is this?" she asked.

OK, maybe she needed me, too. She wasn't recognizing any of this as food. I set the plate on the table and was excited to teach her something that wasn't incredibly awful like the Orkain or the fact that her government had thrown her on an unknown planet under the expectation that they'd be raped or taken advantage of.

"This is vyg." I pulled the fruit apart with my fingers. It was orange and juicy with a pit in the middle. I pulled some fruit off and put a pinch in my mouth. I offered it to her. She didn't seem to know what to do. She offered her hand in the shape of a cup. I continued to hold it gently in my fingers. She gave me a skeptical look and shook her head. I grinned but did as she requested and dropped the wetness in her hand.

It immediately disintegrated without the support of my fingers, the skin having been opened, all of the juices came out into her hand. She giggled. Her giggle was so cute. She took it in stride, gave a little shrug, and then tried to slurp it. She seemed to have good control of her tongue, but there was only one. Her lips pursed together. Her eyes brightened in surprise.

"It's…tangier…than I expected," she said. "It looks sort of like fruit, and our fruit is sweeter."

"This isn't your fruit," I said simply. "Do you not like it, though?"

"Maybe if I wasn't licking it off my hand. How did you get your piece?" she asked.

I pinched the fruit from casing to pit again. I offered it to her. She paused for a moment and then her sweet lips parted for me and accepted my fingers. I swallowed at the same time that she did. Goodness, this might be difficult. I'd had plenty of interactions with women, but she was strange and gorgeous and simply, wonderful. Still, 'plenty of interactions' wasn't that many in a world like my own, and those women had possibly just wanted to rule the population or gain status. This woman was different. She had traveled here just to experience new things, which was admirable, and if only I could be like that, but I had too many responsibilities. I had an entire population to take care of. She could just float off and visit strange worlds and make strange people feel…strange.

"Are you OK?" she asked. I realized I was lost in my thoughts. A wrinkle set between her eyes as she drew her eyebrows together in concern. It was cute, given how smooth her face was otherwise.

"Yes, sorry." What was I going to tell her? Your lips are turning me on? Or, that I'm so used to being alone in this house that I can't stay focused our conversation? I might as well be atop my home, staring at the stars.

"Like this?" she asked as she gingerly pulled on the soft fruit that I held in my hand. Her fingers were so slender. She didn't pinch through the skin at first, then, suddenly, the fruit shot from my hand, squirting us both as it escaped.

After the initial shock, we both laughed out loud, really loud.

"No, not like that," I said, as I picked up the fruit and set it in the sink. "Let's try something else."

I was going to have a lot of fun showing her my world. It was for cultural exchange after all. Maybe even if my population didn't survive, we could at least share our knowledge with others, and some part of us would continue.

"What's your favorite on here?" she asked, glancing over the plate, unsure of what she would like. I could tell she was trying not to make assumptions, but she wasn't doing a good job.

"This is vega. It's from the same plant as the vyg. It's also not sweet, though," I added. I decided it better not to add, 'like your lips.'

I pinched off a darker, fibrous leaf, and was much surprised when she opened her mouth. She must have read my face, because she blushed even if she didn't change her mind and close her mouth. I pretended not to make a big deal of it and placed it into her mouth, partly on her tongue so she could immediately taste it.

"Oh wow," she said, chewing on it. "It's sort of…meaty."

I didn't understand that word, but I nodded anyway. I took my own piece. It didn't have the tangy juice of the fruit. It was savory and fulfilling. If one was thirsty, vyg made the most sense, but if one was hungry, I thought that vega made much more sense as a food choice, even though I guess they both did the same at the end.

"You don't talk much, do you?" she asked, and I realized I was conversing in my head more than with my guest, again.

"I'm sorry. It's sad, but we've been living alone and apart for so long, that I get sort of lost in my own world."

"Oh, I get that. I stopped working for a bit, and I lived by myself. If it wasn't for my sister, I think I would have forgotten how to talk altogether," she said with an understanding smile. It had a bit of sadness underneath it, too.

"It doesn't help that this isn't my first language. I don't mean that to be rude. It's just, I think in one language and then have to translate it—"

"Thank you," she interrupted.

"For what?"

"For learning our language. I mean, I assume it was difficult. We humans don't easily learn languages. You did that for our comfort, and that's wow, that's really nice."

I was glad to be thought so noble. We were so much more desperate than that, though. Learning a language was a small price to pay to possibly continue our people. We were already at the brink of disaster. Already, some things were not going to survive past this generation. I had already assumed I would have to relinquish the 'throne' so to speak. The job had been passed down generationally, but I would likely have no heir. It wasn't something needed anyway, anymore. The role had been largely ceremonial when our government had been so large. Now, with so few people, leaders were fewer, and should be chosen based on merit, rather than bloodlines.

"The relationship between our people was—is— important to us. We want you to be happy here, despite pretense."

She shook her head. I wasn't sure what she meant. And, I was too scared to ask for clarification. Languages and generations felt less important in the moment, as did heirs and biological mating. At this time, I only needed Katy to physically stay in my home. I thought she needed me as much as I needed her, but her actions proved otherwise. I wasn't sure how to keep her here, with me.

I decided to go the honest route.

"I'll take you to see your sister when it's safe, but I need you to not run away anymore." She shied, even as she sat on my counter, having just eaten food from my hand. "While the situation is awful, I hope you find some happiness here. You came to experience new things. I'm going to do my best to make sure you have the best experience you can have, if even just to give the best impression of my people and culture before we die out into the abyss."

She sighed. I sensed she was conflicted. "Running off was stupid. I'd be dead if you hadn't found me. I am sorry for your people. For what it's worth, it doesn't seem like you deserve it."

"Oh, we have our mistakes. All people do. I just hope we can recover from them in time to stay around and learn from your people, my people, and maybe eventually, *our people.*"

Katy gave a small smile, but I could tell she wasn't thinking so big picture. She didn't have to. Her world wasn't at stake. She put a piece of food into her mouth and immediately spit it out in surprise at what it tasted like.

I laughed. In this moment my world wasn't at stake either, just this little one where I wanted to give her food she'd actually eat. She was my world right now, and it lived or died by her smile.

Those sweet lips.

If only our fruit tasted as sweet.

If only.

Chapter Eight
Home?

Katy

The food was simple, yet delicious. I was almost enjoying myself. And, I also felt bad for Drex. He was in charge of his dying people, in the midst of a losing war with an alien species, relying on America's government to perhaps change his fate. If our government was capable of anything, it was changes of fates, but not for the better. I was almost starting to believe that Drex hadn't agreed to this program only looking for wombs, even if that's what our government saw the program as. I mean, I had fallen for the bait and switch too, hadn't I? Still, it was difficult for me to get past a belief like that—his people desperately needed wombs. And while he was talking a good talk, we hadn't yet made it past the first day. He would have plenty of time to get impatient and demand things I wouldn't want to give him.

It didn't seem fair to have him worrying about me running away again. I would give him a chance to take me to my sister. She had seemed all right in the call. It wasn't his fault I signed up and shot myself across the skies. I was in a strange place without anything. I was just going to have to play nice.

"And the humans can't live together?" I asked, again. I had been told that wouldn't be the case by my government, too. It was supposed to be a home-guest situation. One of the few things that were true, I guessed.

"No, you're not as hot as our females, but it's still too dangerous."

"Excuse me! That's sort of rude," I said, even though I also believed it to be true.

"What? I'm sorry?"

"You said we weren't as hot as your females. We're a different species, you shouldn't compare."

"It's just true. Our females run at a temperature of…on your scale…110 Fahrenheit? You are less than 100 degrees at the moment."

I laughed again, really laughed.

"It's not funny. That's how the Orkain find them. They are hotter than the males. They've been captured at significantly higher rates."

"No, I'm sorry. It was just a misunderstanding. In my culture, we also use 'hot' to mean 'attractive.' You were saying we weren't 'as hot,' but I thought you were saying that we weren't as good looking."

It was his turn to give a bit of a grin. "No, I think in that regard, you are *very hot*."

I swallowed hard. The way he said that, staring straight into my eyes, super serious, changed the temperature of the room, of my body. And the way he smirked…I caught a glimpse of his tongue. Was it forked?

"May I ask you something? When you laugh…I see your tongue a bit. Does it…look different than mine?" I stuck my tongue out goofily.

He stuck out his.

There were three.

Well, maybe that wasn't quite right. There was one tongue with two smaller strips of muscle on either side, but it was evident from his actions that he could move them all independently. My core gave a twitch that slipped between my legs. I didn't think he meant for it to be sexy, but it totally and completely was. My body felt it before my brain could even register it. It was alien. It was a bit creepy. And it was also hot.

I guess my face revealed my body's reaction, because a smile crept into the corners of his mouth as if he knew. I felt myself flush and look away.

"Despite our differences, it is sort of interesting how much we are alike, having developed on different planets," he said, academically, giving me a chance to recover.

I nodded. I didn't let my mind wander to how much of his anatomy might be like and *not like* human male anatomy. My government had surely investigated and had some inkling that biological mating would be possible.

I was thankful for the food. It was strange, but not gross. I guessed there could be worse things. As long as I got to see my sister often, and no one tried to impregnate me, it might be OK. And then, my sister and I would catch the next rocket out of here.

#

The windows in my room lightened with the morning skies. I wasn't sure if it was artificial or not, but it made for a soft and pleasant awakening. I pulled the blankets tight around my curled body and for a moment, I was home—back in my apartment—content in my bed. As I awakened more fully, reality came crashing in. I wasn't at home. I wasn't even on Earth. Part of me wanted to hide in bed all day, like I'd done for the better part of a year. But curiosity, and the desire to start anew in this strange world, pushed me from my comfortable spot.

Looking through the drawers, I found a snug-fitting tank top, and long pants made of a light fabric. I wished for a way to put my hair up, as I assumed today would be just as warm as yesterday. I guess I'd have to explain "hair bands" to my alien host. For now, I braided my hair and tied the bottom with a ribbon I'd found. It would at least keep it from sticking to my face when I began to sweat, as I knew I would, no matter what job I found to do. That was my goal for today, was to find a way to be a useful and contributing member of Xavian society. Perhaps, under different circumstances, I would have lazed around a bit, but given that we were here for uh, *other* purposes, it felt prudent to get a job. And I was actually excited about the prospect. I had done this to start a new life; it didn't need to wait until I got back to Earth.

When I entered the main living space, I didn't see Drex there or in the kitchen. Maybe he wasn't an early riser, or maybe he had already slipped out to do his work. I didn't know what hours he kept. But as I walked from the kitchen, I saw through the front windows from a different angle. Drex sat on a stool outside, with his back to me. I opened the door and announced a cheery "Good morning."

He started, and I realized that I had disturbed him from some deep train of thought. Otherwise, he would have definitely heard me open the door. He smiled congenially. "Good morning." He stumbled over the words.

"I'm sorry. I interrupted something. Um, what did I interrupt?" I was hoping it wasn't some sort of prayer. What were the chances that we'd be praying to the same idea of God? I wasn't ready to have a deeply philosophical conversation this early in the morning.

"I was convening with the silence of the morning."

"Oh." Okay, I was definitely interrupting the silence.

He motioned me to sit next to him. He had his knees bent and shins stacked on top of each other like logs. I tried to copy his stance, but I found my hips didn't cooperate. I couldn't stack my legs like that. I settled for crisscross, applesauce. I didn't teach him the rhyme or comment on his remarkable flexibility, because *convening with the silence* and all.

He closed his eyes and breathed deeply, and I realized it was a sort of meditation. He didn't hold his hands up with his index finger and thumbs touching. He didn't hum or make any guttural sounds. He was just still and quiet. After a bit, I decided to trust and close my eyes for a moment or two and realized just how quiet it was. There were no birds or animals crying out in the morning. It was silent, save for any movement of water or the movement of plants as the dew dried off them, and they sprung a little closer to the sun. Wow. OK, maybe I was imagining that, but it was still really, really quiet.

There was no such silence on Earth. There was busyness everywhere. We had so many people. So many vehicles. Road traffic. I lived in a city. There were sirens. Here in the morning, there was nothing. And despite the fact that it was like this probably every morning, Drex was appreciating it in a way that made it seem like he knew there were much louder places, and he didn't take his place for granted.

My stomach growled.

He laughed and blinked his eyes open.

"The silence has brought forth hunger. Would you like a meal?"

"Breakfast. It's called 'breakfast.' Do you have a morning meal?"

"No, but that doesn't mean you can't have one. We usually start eating later in the day. What does one eat in the morning?"

"Oh, it depends. I like some sort of bread and coffee, definitely coffee."

"What are those?"

"Ohh," I groaned. The worse part of the question of 'what's coffee' is that he was asking that question. "Coffee is a magical beverage of Earth. We dry the beans of this plant and brew them in hot water, and it makes this drink that energizes you. There's this thing called 'caffeine' in it, and if you drink too much of it, it can make you feel hyper and jittery, but really it just helps you wake up and it's magical. Did I mention it's magical?"

He laughed. "What's magical?"

"Ok, never mind, but, ugh. You've got nothing like that here?"

"No, we do. I'm just teasing you."

"Oh gosh, you're just messing with me?! Really, you have coffee?"

The prince was actually kind of funny…as long as he was joking. I really did want some coffee.

"Yes, the first explorers from your planet were excited when they learned we had something similar to what you call 'coffee.' We call it 'fah.'"

"May I have some faw?"

"Sharper end to the word. Fah."

"Fah."

"Yes, you may."

"I'd also like to help prepare it. I want to learn. And the reason I came out here was to find out what we're doing today. I would like to get a job. I want to earn my keep."

"You want to work?" he asked, a bit incredulously. That apparently wasn't what he thought I would want to do with my time on a remote planet. Perhaps he thought I had left Earth to vacation the whole time, and maybe some had. Probably my sister, Sara, now that I was thinking about it. Being unemployed for so long on Earth had driven me crazy (so crazy I'd flown to a distant planet). I wasn't going to continue that here. I'd get a job, learn some skills, and…whatever they called money here. I was going to earn that too.

I nodded and after a moment he realized I was serious.

"Honestly, I hadn't thought about that. Did you have a job on Earth?"

"I took pictures, photographs? With a camera."

"And that's a job?" he asked.

My face dropped a bit, I think. I didn't think he meant it to be rude. Still, my skin reddened. I guess it seemed like a stupid job here.

"I didn't mean any offense," he said. "We haven't had jobs like that in a generation, but I'm sure we did.

I mean, there are plenty of these…photographs…" he tried the longer word, "I didn't think about the fact that someone was probably paid to take them. They're important. They're history. They tell us what life was like before, and where it could be again, or even better."

He sounded like a politician, but his voice faltered on the last three words, as if he knew no one would believe them. They were hollow. Why even say them? I guessed that was his job.

"Did you photograph anything specific on Earth?" he asked.

"Mostly weddings."

"What are those?"

I twitched at the question and rushed through an explanation. "It's a ceremony where two humans vow to stay together in a romantic relationship and partnership for the rest of their lives."

"Ah, a ceremony for rotha," he said.

"Rotha?"

I recognized the same nervousness from him. Maybe we shared the same feelings on the subject. "My species has a biological reaction to their mate. When they find their partner, there is a strong bond that occurs. We have a ceremony to celebrate it."

"What sort of biological reaction?" I asked.

"It's different for everyone. My parents were rotha partners. My father said he felt a tender pull that stretched his insides. My mother said her heart felt heavy like a stone in her chest. As they spent time together, their zarata chemistry marked them with a pattern on their skin from their wrists to their elbows, but it manifests differently for every pair or group."

"Zarata…that's the second time you've used that term. What is it?"

"I don't know the English word. It's the…spirit of who you are? The essence, or personality but deeper."

"Maybe, soul?" I replied. I was sort of in quiet awe. At first, it sounded like he was just describing romance, puppy love, and excitement in a new relationship, but physical markings appearing was…well, alien. I couldn't help but think that life on Earth would be simpler if there were such plain signs.

"Do people get together that aren't rotha partners?"

"Oh yes, some quite happily, although it's said that fertility is decreased in such cases. I'm not sure if that's true. Either way, it wasn't a big deal at the time. And really, not now, either. With so few people, it seems rotha may be a thing of the past."

He gazed off, seemingly lost in his thoughts. While I had assumed 'trading for females' to be a crude, thoughtless solution; there were costs their society wrestled with of which I had no understanding.

Breaking from his reverie, he asked, "did you ever have your own…wedding?"

Damn. The way he asked the question made it difficult to dodge. If he'd asked if I was married, I could have said honestly no, but I sort of did have a wedding. I just hadn't gotten married. "Uh, I was supposed to be in a wedding, but my fiancé didn't show up on the day of our wedding, so we were never 'married' which is the legal outcome after you do the paperwork and everything."

"What happened? Was he killed?" Drex asked alarmed, and it sort of broke my heart a little bit that he could be so naive. I mean, I guess I had been too.

How could someone be so close to a new life and just ditch?

"No, he just decided not to come," I said, then quickly adjusted in the seat to distract myself from his reaction. My face felt hot and my hands clammy.

"I am sorry," he said. And he seemed genuine about it. Of course, he was. It was an easy thing to feel sorry about. What a horror, but I didn't want it to define me.

"It's okay. Rotha is forever?"

"Practically…yes. There are many biological changes. It puts the couples at a great advantage. I've never known a rotha couple to separate There is fundamentally a biological need. Often, they die within a few months of each other."

"Wow, rotha sounds kind of terrifying," I half-joked. What sort of messed up biology occurs that the spouse just up and dies if they lose the other one? I had heard it in old people who were having health issues anyway…dying from a broken heart, but this seemed like something, well, alien.

"When did this wedding not happen?" Drex asked. He tried to ask nonchalantly, but I could tell he was very interested in the answer.

"About a year ago."

Drex had learned the passage of time on Earth and its measurements from my government. He nodded, looking at the ground thoughtfully. I eyed the door in the awkward moment. He'd think I'd gotten on that rocket to get away from that situation. I mean, I guess, I had.

"Yep, turns out I got baggage," I said.

He looked at me curiously. Another colloquialism. I clarified. "Ah, 'emotional baggage.' Carrying around a history, some pain, not a blank slate."

He seemed to understand. "Our histories and pain color us, but how we choose to move from there is our zarata. You are strong. I have no doubt."

Maybe it was our physical distance from the wedding and the planet it was on. Maybe it was lost in translation, but for the first time, someone had listened to my trauma, accepted it, and gave me space to move on from it. It was strange and freeing at the same time.

"Come, let me teach you about fah."

"Thank you," I said, and I meant it for more than just the fah.

Inside the kitchen, he pulled out a jar of what looked like dried plant leaves and unsealed it. The smell of sweet jasmine filled the air.

"It's tea!" My excitement immediately began to fade as I remembered jasmine tea on Earth didn't have caffeine. Apparently going cold-turkey for three months was long enough to kick the caffeine addiction I'd nursed for the last twenty-something years.

"That's what they said. What's the difference, again?"

"Coffee is a fruit from a specific plant. It's roasted dry. Tea can be the dried leaves or flowers or fruit from many different plants. It has more variety. Some of it is caffeinated—like coffee, it has a particular substance that's basically a stimulant to humans. Some of it isn't." I said the last part with a bit of down in my voice.

"I'm sure you'll find this perfectly stimulating." He folded the leaf in half to crease it before pulling it apart. He then repeated the process to one of the halves. "I'll start you with half strength. I don't want you…what was it? Jattery?"

"Jittery, and sure." I had been so tolerant to caffeine for so long that I was actually pretty excited that there was a chance I could feel those jitters again. Boy, my behavior was 'still addicted' even if my body wasn't physically. Apparently, stasis didn't break bad habits. What I wouldn't do for a caramel macchiato with an extra shot of espresso. I could make some good coffee at home. I had my own machines. Caffeine was important for a freelancer, and I always had a thermos attached to my hip along with my camera.

He filled a kettle-looking thing with water from the sink. He pressed a button on it, and in just a moment, the water was steaming, then boiling.

"Wow," I said. "I like that."

He smiled. "Hot."

He was talking about the kettle, but my body involuntarily responded to the word coming out of his mouth. I wasn't sure which meaning of 'hot' he meant, but apparently, I registered another meaning when it was spoken by a sexy man making me fah in the kitchen.

He pulled out two handle-less cups that were thick stone, and then put them in what looked like an oven. While they were warming or whatever, he rolled the leaves between his fingers. They formed cylindrical shapes which he returned to the counter. He pulled out the mugs with his bare hands so they couldn't be too hot, but I was still going to be careful not to burn myself. He poured water into the mugs. And then motioned me closer. I took a few steps closer, and I wasn't sure if the heat was radiating off the teas or off his body, or both, I guess. I do know my heart beat quicker close to him. The scent in the air was thick with spice. *Boy, get it together, Katy*, I told myself. *The man is just making you a drink.* I tried to watch the tea process, but to be honest I was pretty distracted. He wore the same loose linen fabric which seemed to drape over his muscles rather than clothe him. We needed that sort of material on Earth, not whatever stupid mineral the government was looking for. Drex looked *good.*

I willed myself to bring the teas into actual focus, instead of focusing on the peripheral. It wasn't working. Drex also seemed to be hesitating, too. Was my proximity affecting him too? I looked up into his face and saw he was blushing a bit. What would he be blushing about? I let my eyes fall down his body, with the excuse that I was looking back down at the teas, and then I saw what he might find blush-worthy. In fact, I was sort of surprised he had blood to color his face, for the large bulge that was threatening to ram the kitchen counter. It stretched his pants, and I could tell that he was quite um, long. He wasn't close to the counter, but *it* was. I think I gave a little gasp, because when I looked back up, he gave a sheepish grin.

"I apologize," he said. "I'll wear um, some different pants when you're around."

"It's not a big deal," I said, which was a complete lie. It was definitely by any definition, *a big deal.* But I could be mature about it. "As long as you don't try anything," I said, even as I dismissed the same thoughts.

"Of course. I promise I'm respectful of you and your boundaries. My body is reacting to your presence, but I can control my actions."

"I get it. You don't have many women around here," I tried to brush it off.

"No, it's not that. I'm around women all the time because of my job. You're um…special."

Yeah, special in that you thought I had flown millions of light years to mount you. I then had to distract myself from the image of mounting him. We took a couple of moments to gather ourselves before remembering the tea. He dropped the rolled leaf into the mug, and I watched the heat and water expand the leaf into a spiral that floated vertically in the cup. It was simple and beautiful. He handed me the drink. "Don't drink it yet. You have to let the leaf infuse with the water."

The cup was super heavy and warm. I cradled it with both hands. He motioned for me to sit at the table by the kitchen, as he began pulling things out of the cupboard, presumably for my breakfast. I obediently went over to the table but felt out of place. I wasn't used to someone serving me. I felt I should make my own breakfast if he didn't even eat the meal, but I didn't know where…or what…anything was. It made sense he was brushing off my desire for a job. What was I going to manage?

"How do you know when to take the leaf out?" I asked, thinking about tea on Earth.

"You don't. It melts or dissolves…I'm not really sure what the correct term in your language is. By that time the water has cooled to a nice temperature too, I think, but others wait longer. Just be careful."

I would be. He ran warm. He probably could tolerate hotter environmental temperatures than me as well.

I watched it dissolve in the cup, while still trying to keep an eye on Drex. I wanted to be able to ask him questions about what he was doing so maybe I could start taking care of myself here. I'd still work on trying to get him to let me have a job, but at least I could make sure he didn't have to work *and* take care of me.

I hated feeling helpless. It reminded me of that wretched failed wedding day. I never wanted to feel that helpless again. And for the most part, besides my employment issue, I hadn't had to ask for help yet. That was why I was here. I was going to make the best decisions for me only, not for any relationship or man. My sister was the only other person that would be able to sway me like that again, and I trusted her. She'd never just not show up.

The leaf was barely visible. The cup emitted the smell of spearmint and jasmine. It was heavenly and I let the steam envelop my face and fill my lungs for a moment. It was still clearly too hot for me to drink, but I saw that Drex was swirling his cup to encourage the last of his leaf to finish and then took a giant swig.

"Ack, leaf still," he said, and pulled a tiny scrap off one of his tongues.

I laughed.

He gave an embarrassed smile. "I'm always taking the first sip too soon."

"It's handy that it dissolves though. With our tea and coffee, you have to remove the material. If you leave it in too long it gets bitter."

"If you can wait that long," he joked.

With some of the sexual tension relaxing, I retried our previous conversation. "I do want a job," I said. I wasn't about to let that go. My government had lied about so much, while I couldn't yet even think about the idea that they wouldn't be coming back...that would send me into some sort of spiral...I could at least prepare to be here for a while and that definitely required a job.

"You don't need a job. That's the benefit of a host. I'm *hosting* you," he said. He seemed a little offended, even.

"I don't want to be some bum…" I wanted to affirm I was more than a womb, or fun-seeking tourist. I needed to work. I wasn't sure how to make him understand.

He sighed. "I mean, maybe later, or if you were with a different host. It feels like a step backward if the prince's mate is sent out to work—"

"MATE?"

He stammered. "Just that's how it's going to look to my people. I'm hosting you, a potential mate… I'm sorry, that slipped, but do you see what I'm saying? What you do sets precedent for all humans."

"We should work if we're going to be here long," I said, fuming a bit, matching my drink. He wasn't going to let me work, because of *his* job title?

"You're too precious to work," he said.

I couldn't believe I'd gotten so hot and flustered just a few moments earlier. There was no way I was just going to sit around as a princess and be fed grapes all day, but I let it go for now. He began preparing my food, and I abandoned my cup so that I could watch and learn how to prepare the food. I demanded to know what everything was. He was patient with me, but he could tell I was still upset.

By the time I got back to my cup of fah, it was cold. He offered to make me a new cup, but I refused, drinking it down fast. The flavors were pretty intense, herbal. It could use some sweetener and some creamer, but I didn't ask for anything like those things. I was going to ask for as little as possible until I figured out how to stop this incurring landslide of social debt.

"I have several people to meet today. I'll be out of the house. Is there anything you'd like me to show you before I leave? Would you like to bathe?" He didn't say it rudely. It was just an offer.

I nodded.

"Are you going to be OK here by yourself? Are you going to run away again?" This time his voice was a little tight. I think I made him nervous. Good. He should be nervous. I'm not his and he should wonder what I'm going to do, because I'm my own person.

I smiled. "I'll be here when you get back," I said.

His eyes narrowed a bit as he realized that I hadn't promised I wouldn't leave. I wouldn't, though. There were things I could do here. I planned to sort the clothes I would wear from the clothes I wouldn't. That way they could be returned from wherever they had come from or could go to some of the other women. Maybe we could do some sort of clothes and supply swap.

"When can you escort me back to the ship? I have personal things on it."

"We can arrange that. Davian mentioned that many of the women expressed the need to return to the ship for things. He is going to coordinate it so that we won't be amassing there all at once. Maybe even have the items delivered, if we can figure out what's what. That way we can keep you all safe. We also have to find out if the Orkain are watching the ship. It is a strange thing that arrived, and they have already found prey there."

I noticed he called us 'women' this time instead of 'mates,' although then, 'prey.' I'd rather he called us humans and not identify us by our gender. I couldn't be too picky because we were going to be a helpless group at their mercy for a while.

"Please don't try to go to the ship without me. If you have to go right now, I will go with you right now. Please just don't go alone," he was almost pleading, but I wasn't sure if that was because he wanted to keep me safe or if it was because he was worried about the optics of the prince being the first to lose his stupid human mate. The very thought made me angry, but he was also right. Even if I wanted to go by myself, I had no idea where the ship was. I would get lost immediately again.

I begrudgingly nodded and just let him worry about my actions even if I had no plans for leaving. I just wanted him to think I could leave. Keep him on his toes. *That's right, buddy. I'm my own person, and I can be as stupid as I want.*

"All right, let me show you the bathing room," he said. He moved to clear the table, and I put my hands out to stop him.

"Nah, I saw where everything came from. I'll wash it and put it back. It'll give me something to do."

He opened his mouth to protest but then thought better of it. "I guess it'll keep you busy so you won't run away again." Then a big smile erupted on his face.

He was still sort of a jerk, though.

Drex showed me the bathing room which wasn't entirely alien and was actually quite luxurious. They had running hot water and had little need to conserve water. He showed me the shower, and its multiple shower heads, and how to adjust the temperature. It was slate and glass. There was a small personal tub that was empty, and a small soaking pool that was deep and large enough for a couple of people. "We put these in with the new houses, because you can't do hot tubs outside anymore," he said.

That made sense. I didn't know if they were in all the houses, or if he was rich as the prince and thus had some extra goodies in his home. Anyway, it seemed nice. I planned to take a shower and then soak in it for a few minutes before drying off. Eventually, Drex had to leave, and I got to experience the shower.

It was definitely better than any shower I'd had on Earth. It measured where my head was and showered everything but my face pretty much all the time. It felt weird at first, but it turned out to be nice. None of those cold spots or always moving around to keep yourself wet and warm. The heat felt good on my skin and comforted me. Drex had one dispenser of soap that he used for his entire body. I didn't know if that was an alien thing or if that was a male thing, but it did seem to wash and rinse from my hair. We'd see how it looked when it dried. I wondered if any of the women that came with us was a hair dresser. My sister and I had trimmed each other's hair as it had grown long in stasis, but it wasn't the same as getting it styled. The female aliens here had different hair styles and textures; I wasn't sure they'd be able to cut it how I liked it. Perhaps I would have to learn. A stabbing thought hurt as I realized my ways of learning things, looking it up online, streaming videos, even just plain magazines and books, were all not accessible to me anymore. That was a scary thought, and I skirted around it by turning off the water and stepping out of the shower.

Now clean, I felt comfortable getting in the plunge pool. It was warm and steaming, and it was a delight on my skin that was quickly cooling from the shower. Drex had set the temperature a bit lower for me, knowing that my body temperature was even lower than his. He wanted me to be comfortable. That was thoughtful, but then again, a lot of his culture focused on body temperature given the threat in the skies. I had to remind myself not to misread some of the things he was doing as special consideration; he was very respectful, though.

I'm not sure how long I soaked in the pool. It was nice to float in something as familiar as water. Everything here was so different, but this felt like a spa. I could get used to this. Eventually, the steam in the room began to make me a bit dizzy, so I reluctantly got out. There were thick, soft towels, and after drying off, I wrapped myself in one and risked crossing the hall to get to my bedroom. Drex had left and wouldn't be back for most of the day.

Once in my room, I locked my door, just in case. My hair had mostly dried except for the ends which had been floating in the pool. I dabbed them with the towel until they didn't drip anymore. Then I began trying on clothes that I wasn't sure about their fit. Eventually, I had the clothes sorted that I would keep and clothes that I would tell Drex that I wouldn't use. After, I put on another tunic and cinched it around my waist. The underwear was more comfortable than Earth underwear, less binding elastic, but they still stayed up. Since I was still by myself, I didn't put on pants. I was still pretty modest looking, and as someone who lived by myself, I didn't wear pants in the house often. Old habits died hard.

I folded the clothes I wanted to keep and organized them in the drawers. There was enough for a couple of weeks without washing, depending on what I wanted to wear, but I would have to get Drex to teach me how to do laundry here. I hoped they had machines for it. Goodness, what if they didn't? They had a dishwasher.

I'm sure they had laundry machines. I imagined Sara screaming as she ran off if she discovered otherwise. I hoped she was living in the lap of luxury. This was her stupid idea. I was going to demand to see her when he came back tonight.

I folded the clothes I wouldn't be using and stacked them up at the end of my very long bed. Now what was I going to do?

Chapter Nine
Frustnerrd

Drex

So now I understood more fully why Katy had traveled across the vast reaches of space. It wasn't to connect to someone. It was to distance herself from the situation she had at home. I knew there would be complex reasons why someone would take such a risk like this, but I guessed I hadn't reconciled it with someone I would be with. She still sounded hurt. It was difficult for her to speak about it. I wanted to take that pain away from her, but it was not something that could be done. Rotha was for life, maybe even longer. Her pain wouldn't resolve until she was together again with her rotha mate.

While I typically did my work from my office in the house, I decided to leave to give Katy some space and privacy. I figured she would feel safer that way. And honestly, I needed some time to process the things that had happened as well. I met with Vance in one of the abandoned store fronts of Frustnerrd. Unfortunately, we knew the Orkain would be less likely to be out, given their successful hunt last night.

"This is the best idea you've ever had," said Vance. The smile he had on before the arrival of the women had returned.

"Meeting in a store?" I asked. We sat cross-legged on the countertop. There weren't any chairs in the establishment, a general store with various items. All of the buildings had been left unlocked, in case someone needed to rush in for cover.

"No, the women. Sara is absolutely gorgeous. I cannot stop staring at her."

I hoped for Sara's benefit that he occasionally stopped staring at her. "Remember, they didn't come here to have sex with us. Please be respectful." I knew he would, but it didn't hurt to remind him.

"Uh, the thing is—I think Sara might have," he smirked.

"You think she knew about the program?" This was news to me, that some of the women might have been aware of the circumstances.

"No, I think she was just planning on having relations with some sexy aliens while vacationing…and I don't mind being one of those aliens."

I shook my head, like Katy had taught me. It seemed appropriate.

I understood where he was coming from, though. Katy's soft body was so very…distracting. I was mesmerized by her shape. I wished to touch it, be close to it, taste it. Honestly, it had less to do with the continuation of the species and more about how my body physically reacted to her. And, he was right; just because they hadn't initially agreed to a reproduction program, didn't mean they wouldn't find it amenable later. I had to keep myself in check. There was already an impossible public relations issue here. Any impolite behavior would form into a fierce scandal. All the men selected to host had been extensively vetted by myself, many who I knew personally, that were willing to put aside the species' needs and their own desires to keep the respect of a woman. Anyone here would be like that. It was amazing that the Earth's government had ever thought otherwise. Is that how women were treated on their planet?

"You're not getting that impression from yours?"

"She's not *mine*. She's a guest. Her name is Katy."

"Right, right. You're not getting that impression from Katy?"

"No, she seems more concerned about her sister. They seem pretty close." I considered telling Vance more about Katy's escape attempt, but I was already feeling pretty inept in the situation. His supposed progress he was making with Katy's sister didn't make me feel any better about it. I settled with, "I think I need to help her feel more comfortable."

"You're not going to do that by leaving her alone all the time. We should be working from home. Instead of sitting here on this uncomfortable glass counter."

"I guess I've gotten used to being by myself," I admitted.

"But you're here with me. I think *you* need to become more comfortable with her."

Vance had a point. I would make a point to remain at the house and get to know my company. There should be less pressure at this point. She wasn't here to mate. She was here to be close to her sister. This could actually work out. She didn't have any expectations of me. She just expected I respect her. I could do that.

"Speaking of work, has Davian submitted further reports on the guest situation?" I asked.

"While it's unfortunate that an Orkain took off with one of the women, I think it's scared a lot of the women into staying put."

"And they're satisfied with their rooms and their hosts?"

"Yes. They're anxious to stay with someone who speaks English with them. They hadn't been given any lessons in Xavian. It was another good decision on your part," said Vance.

The Earth government was a frustrating system. Had they really thought that dropping off clueless females would solve our problems? Did they think they'd just…what did they think we were going to do with them? Well, we were going to treat them better than their own government. That was for sure. I had required all of the hosts to learn English so that their guests would feel welcome and comfortable. Humans used mostly verbal language, and I wanted to do that for them. Even Xavians outside of the government and hosting programs had learned a great deal of English. We would give them places to live until the Earth government came back for their holmium and for those who didn't want to stay. Although, I wasn't sure if I'd want to go back to a planet that treated me like that, myself.

#

After my meeting with Vance, I stopped at one of the other stores in Frustnerrd. When my parents organized us to go underground, we had abandoned the entire town. It was too early for things to have deteriorated; there was still inventory in the stores, flyers for old events in the windows. Its emptiness was eerie, though. Even though I wasn't the one who had ordered the evacuation, I looked at the continued vacancy as a professional failure of mine. I hadn't been able to get us back. If this alliance with the humans did not work out, the evacuation would have only been a provisional measure—a delay to our people's demise.

So needless to say, I didn't like spending a lot of time in Frustnerrd, but I had a gift idea for Katy. I hoped it would make her feel more comfortable and less likely to run away from my home. I found a handheld settit, a personal communicator that Katy could use to talk to her sister from the privacy of her room. I picked up a second to give to Vance to give to Sara. The two of them would be able to talk whenever they wanted. I quickly made my way home, knowing I probably shouldn't leave her alone too long. This woman stressed me out.

I was pleased to see her in the clothes that we had provided her, instead of that uncomfortable-looking space outfit. She had a neatly folded stack of clothes on the urish, or couch as she called it, where she sat puzzling over an almanac that previously sat on my table. I glanced over her shoulder at the dry text.

"I have no idea what it says," she confessed. "I was hoping for some pictures."

She closed the book and smiled up at me. I sensed the smile was a little forced, but at least she tried. I would do my best, too. Things were bound to be uncomfortable before we could relax. It was a strange situation!

"I've got mostly village records and histories here, nothing exciting," I explained.

"Thank you for the clothes. I've brought out what won't fit. Maybe they can go to another woman here," she suggested.

"That's a great idea. Thank you. I got you something." I pulled the settit from my bag.

"Oh, thank you. What is it?" She looked at her reflection in it and brushed some of her hair back behind her ear. Unbidden, I thought of touching it myself to see if it was as soft as it appeared. I refrained.

"It's a smaller version of the settit I have in my office. I've got one to give to Sara, so you can communicate with her whenever you want."

"Wow, really?!" she said, jumping up. She almost dropped it. She recovered and laughed. She smiled a genuine smile, and my heart leaped.

"Yep, I'll show you how it works," is what I said, but all I could think about was how I could keep her this happy. It felt really good.

Chapter Ten
Seeing Sara

Katy

Several days passed before we were allowed to revisit the ship, escorted. I was one of the first to go. I didn't want to get special treatment simply because I was being hosted by the prince, nor did I want to "owe" him anything, but after others with specific, time-sensitive reasons retrieved their things, I didn't have any more excuses. They had to do it in some order, and I didn't have a reason why I should or shouldn't go at any particular time. Drex took off the morning to go with me, and I was happy to go outside, even if I was a bit nervous about the Orkain.

"There haven't been any sightings this morning, either of the Orkain or of your ship," he said as if reading my mind. Maybe he saw me glancing up at the sky. Sure, I was a bit nervous that a demon was going to grab me with its hawk-talons, but I was also mesmerized by their moons floating in the sky with the sun. I had enjoyed any time I could see the moon during daytime on Earth. It had always felt a little mysterious. I was sure the moons had a different rate of appearance here, maybe even all the time, but it was all new to me.

I hadn't even considered the Earth ship. I had given up on it landing and telling us this had all been a mistake. I was stuck here for the year, and I was starting to accept it. Drex had given me a small settit, and I was able to talk to my sister every afternoon. Her evenings were reserved for Vance. I was surprised how well they seemed to be getting along. And Drex and I were getting along, too. Perhaps the time would pass uneventfully and not be too awful, but then I was going home. There was no way I would stay here with the crazy devil Orkain. I was going home where the worst things I had to deal with were raising my credit score and what to binge-watch on Netflix.

"If you don't mind, I'm going to take you a different way. I thought you would like to stop and see your sister."

His suggestion completely surprised me. I squealed and gave him a big hug. Or, tried to. I could barely reach his shoulders. He was so tall. It wasn't until I could smell his warm musk mingling with the scent of the body soap (which I had learned was called soaff) that I realized I was so close to him.

It seemed to surprise him, too. I felt something jump in his pants.

Oops.

"Yes, thank you," I said, moving away from him quickly. I didn't want to embarrass him. I was already embarrassed. His hands lingered on my arms maybe a moment longer than they needed to, although he didn't try to pull me back to him or anything. Instead, he chuckled, then we sort of awkwardly continued down the path. He showed me different plants, telling me their names. He seemed to have good knowledge of nature. I would not be able to do the same for him on Earth. I lived in the city. Plants came either cut and labeled as different vegetables in the store or cut as flowers in expensive wedding arrangements. Sure, I could spot a hydrangea, lily, or asteria. I had white hydrangea at my wedding. I loved the big white fluffy flowers. From what I saw here, they had similar poufs of red and orange. I had already forgotten the name Drex had called them, but I thought they were my favorite.

Actually, if I were to be honest, I was still thinking about his scent and his arms. I didn't think anyone would blame me. I had literally never seen someone so strong or so handsome. As a photographer, I've taken photos of models for magazines, but none of them seemed so, I don't know, as *solid* as Drex. The models were toned because they didn't have fat on their bodies. Drex was strong because he worked every day. Like, maybe how you'd think a farmer would look— but not how farmers actually looked. I trusted him to not only have the strength, but the skill and agility to protect me. And it wasn't difficult to imagine those strong arms which had pulled me to safety, to maybe be holding me close.

We were up on the house's porch before I even realized we were even near a house. I never would have been able to find this place on my own.

"Why don't you have road signs?" I asked, "Are you afraid that the Orkain will learn how to read?"

He laughed. "I guess we didn't think about it. We are such a small group now that everyone sort of knows where everything is, but you're right. We now have a bunch of people that don't know. Do you think we should fix it?"

"I think it will make people feel safer and be able to navigate better."

"I don't know if I want any of our guests walking around on their own, for their safety, but we can talk about it. Actually, Vance has an idea about a tunnel system—"

"Are you guys going to knock or what?!" shouted Sara from inside the house.

I laughed. It brought me so much joy to hear her sounding safe and happy. The door burst open. I barely got a look at her before she attacked me with a giant bear hug that was a bit tight, even for me. I coughed, and she let me go, but just hardly, keeping me in her arms.

"Isn't this place amazing?!" she asked, but it seemed rhetorical. I wasn't sure about that. Didn't she remember the giant demons that might take her away? Of course, she hadn't gone out and encountered one by herself, I was sure. I was suddenly embarrassed I had done that. It wasn't something I would have wanted her to do. I was here to protect her and to keep her from doing something stupid, and here I had made the mistake.

As I figured, she didn't wait for me to answer about the amazing-ness of the place. She swung me around into the house which was set up similar to Drex's but the furnishings were quite different. While Drex's was sleek modern, this was cozier with textures and fabrics and tapestries which softened the entire house.

"This is Vance!" she shouted, she grabbed his shoulders and swung into his arms, like they had been together for years. She was apparently quite comfortable with Vance; she always got close fast to her boyfriends. She'd fall flat-out and hard. And then, I'd have to pick up the pieces after the whirlwind romance. I couldn't help but give Vance a look as I didn't expect anything different, even from an interspecies romance. He seemed to take it as a protective older sister stance and pressed into the space with a broad smile.

Vance was a lighter green than Drex. The screen hadn't betrayed that. Sara hadn't undraped herself from his body, and she nonchalantly let her fingers graze along his horns, which were darker and smoother than Drex's horns. I didn't know what kind of feeling they had in those horns if any, but the motion seemed sensual, and I averted my eyes. My sister smiled, like she knew a secret I didn't.

"It seems you two are getting along well," said Drex. Even he couldn't miss how they seemed physically attached to each other. It wasn't difficult to imagine that they'd been like that all night into the morning. Sara's hair was a bit tussled. They both gave sheepish grins. One planet or another, it was all the same. Good sex was good sex.

Honestly, I was a little annoyed. Our government had dropped us off to have sex with these men, and my sister's promiscuity made her seem complicit. While I was attracted to Drex, bedding him felt like indulging in the government's sex trafficking scheme. It was almost a matter of pride. I knew that my sister would argue the opposite. Doing what we wanted—whatever that was—eschewed the government's control.

It seemed a stupid question to ask Sara if she was okay. She would, of course, say that she was. She looked like she was glowing. Principles aside, I was more worried about their first disagreement over something. Vance was strong, and I hoped he had no history of violence. My sister hadn't been a stranger to such things, unfortunately. I understood the hosts had been chosen for their…vitality…they needed to be strong to protect their people from the Orkain, but the powerful physiques also seemed too good to be true. Those muscles rippling under soft fabric weren't just for enjoyment. They could seriously hurt Sara.

"Come have some fah on our back porch," said Sara. '*Our*' didn't skip my recognition. She was already considering this her place.

Thankfully the men held back and talked in the main living room. She handed me a mug of fah, already dissolved, and we stepped out onto a back lanai. Drex did not have one, just a larger front porch. I think I enjoyed having both. Their lanai looked out into a beautiful, manicured garden. "Who knew that big guy likes flowers?" laughed Sara, as she gestured to many of the wild flowers Drex had shown me along the way, but now meticulously grown and sculpted. Even the orange and yellow hydrangea-like poufs were there.

"They're beautiful," I admitted.

"He has a delicate touch," said Sara with a sly smile on her face.

I rolled my eyes at my sister. She was gossiping over our fah on an alien planet as easily as if we were on my couch with a bottle of red wine.

"Have you had sex with yours yet?" she asked.

"That's not what they're here for!" I said in a rushed loud whisper.

"It's…kind of…what they're here for." Her face and shoulders scrunched up in a playful way.

"We are not staying here, Sara." I felt like a mother reminding their child they couldn't buy whatever toy they were carrying in the store.

"Okay, but we're basically here on an extended vacation. Don't waste your time. Have some fun. Seriously…sex that dude up. You are *not* going to regret it." She shook her head and stared off into the distance in awe. "They have—"

Sara didn't finish her sentence as Drex and Vance stepped out onto the lanai. Instead, she just gave me a smile and an enthusiastic nod, as if that explained everything. I didn't know how she was going to finish her sentence, but I understood the subtext behind it.

"Don't let us interrupt," said Vance, even as he picked up Sara so she could sit in his lap.

I tried not to roll my eyes. "No, it's okay. We better be on our way. It's my turn to get my stuff from the ship," I said, standing up.

Vance gave a sly smile that I figured meant he was happy to get back to whatever they were doing before our visit. As silly as my sister was, I felt like the silly one for having such an awkward distance between me and 'my alien.' Their togetherness made me feel like we were doing something wrong. Meanwhile, I hadn't even thought of us as a 'we' until we'd gotten here. We definitely weren't them.

Sara giggled and told me to suit myself. "I'm not even going back there to get my stuff," she said. She gestured at some of the things Vance had given her, including some beautiful jewelry adorning her chest. I wasn't quite ready to give up on my stuff like her. That stuff was mine, and I wouldn't feel like I owed anyone by using it.

I gave her another hug. Vance and Drex exchanged hugs and a few words. It wasn't until we were out of sight of their house that a hardness caught in my throat. Past my annoyance of the sibling-sort, I was really happy to see her alive and doing well. I had felt like a failure when all this fell apart, like I should have known. I was glad it was working out, though. I choked down a small noise of emotion, but ever-tending Drex heard me.

"Are you OK?" he asked, stopping to search my face.

I sort of wished he wasn't always so attentive. I wasn't always ready to express the things I wanted or needed. But I did want to express my gratitude. "Yes, just…thank you. Thank you for taking me to see my sister."

"Of course. She seems to be doing well, right?" he laughed.

I laughed behind a tear or two that had fallen. She *did* look like she was doing well. "I just didn't realize how relieved I'd be to see her."

"I didn't realize either. I would have brought you sooner. I was really just thinking you needed time to recover." He didn't say from what, but I knew he meant my misadventure.

"Thank you for coming after me. I'm sorry I ran off like that," I had apologized before, but now that I had seen my sister—that she was just fine (maybe too fine) and didn't need my help—I realized how stupid I had been.

To my surprise, he drew me into a hug. I allowed my head to settle onto his chest. His arms wrapped around my small frame and, wow, I felt safe and happy. My hands found his back which felt just as solid, strong, and protective as his front. "I'm glad you're okay," he said. "I was scared that something was going to happen to you."

He could have meant that in a diplomatic way. Of course, it would be upsetting if one of his people's guests wandered off and got themselves killed. It was bad PR, but I didn't think that's what he meant. I could tell by the hug. He had been worried about *me*. And I found I cared about him. I looked into his eyes and tried to reassure him I'd be more careful. We were having a nice moment, but then the hug lost some of its magic. Drex pushed away awkwardly. With a glance, I realized it was so I wouldn't feel intruded upon by his large member which was making its presence known. "I wanted to show you something."

I instantly raised my head to look him in the face. My cheeks turned red.

"Oh gosh," he said, copying one of my exclamations. "Not that! No, uh, look." He motioned to the environment around us of which I had completely lost focus.

Our trail followed a small riverbank. There was a stream just a few feet below us. The water was perfectly clear showing the smooth stones underneath and small minnow-like fish darting about. Now I could hear the bubbling of water, and the rustling of leaves in the wind. It was beautiful.

"I thought you'd like to see some scenery other than the jungle trails."

"You thought right, wow, Sara was right. It is amazing here," and I really thought that. The tropical plants were glossy and green, draping over crystal-clear water. He took my hand, and we stepped down onto some rocks to get closer to the water. He slipped off his shoes, sat on a rock, and sunned his face while his feet hung in the water. I suddenly very much wanted my camera. I wanted to capture this moment. I wanted to capture him here, just like this. He gave me a smile and patted the rock, and I sat down next to him. I didn't have to worry about my own shoes because my feet didn't reach the water. He put his arm behind me, and I rested my back on it. It felt good to be close to him. It was as if seeing Sara and Vance had let us know that nothing horrible was going to happen if we touched. And it was true; nothing horrible happened. In fact, it was pretty nice.

"When we get my camera, can we come back here?" I asked. If not now, then later. I didn't want this moment only in my memories. I wanted others to see it. And I hadn't felt that way about photography in a long while. Maybe I needed a new world. Or maybe I just needed some new hope.

"Of course. I've been actually meaning to ask you about that. You brought your camera?"

"I did," I didn't know where he was going with this. I couldn't anticipate it.

"I was thinking that would be an excellent job for you here. We don't have anyone to capture our culture in photos anymore." He looked a bit distantly into the water, even though it wasn't deep. "If our culture is going to disappear with us. I'd like for it to be documented somehow. A sort of small legacy if anyone cared. At the very least, they can learn from our mistakes. What would you think of that job?"

"Wow," was all that escaped me. I didn't think he was going to take me seriously about work, especially when he initially laughed, but now what he was asking of me I didn't even feel capable of. I was both honored and terrified to document his people and their way of life. There had to be better qualified people, especially within his community, but he was asking me. And I wasn't one to say no to a job. "Wow, I'll try my best. Thank you. Thank you so much."

And then I don't know what came over me, but I leaned forward and put my lips on his.

At first, he didn't respond. I moved my lips just a bit more, then he did too. Suddenly I realized that aliens might not kiss. I pulled back with wide eyes. I wasn't sure what to do.

"What was that?" he asked innocently.

"That's a kiss," I said. "Do you not have kisses here?"

He shook his head, "but I like it."

He moved his head close to mine, and our lips touched again. The idea of teaching him something new was exciting. And though I wouldn't admit it to him, it was emboldening to perform the act without having any baggage or significance attached to it. My lips parted, and my tongue explored his heated lips. He felt like a furnace. His lips parted too, and I braced myself for three tongues slipping into my mouth. They played with my tongue, inside my lips, and grazed my teeth all at once, gently and tantalizing. I tried not to gasp with my mouth on his. After a few moments, we pulled back at a natural pause, and I looked into his eyes. They twinkled, and his smile brightened his whole face.

"You guys totally have kissing here," I said.

He laughed and nodded.

I tried to push him off the rock and into the water, but he didn't budge. He was strong and heavy. I laughed though. He really had me going there for a second, thinking I was teaching this hunky man how to kiss me. I shook my head.

The joke didn't last long as he was intent on one thing, and that was to kiss me more. I gave him one more gentle kiss before I jumped off the rock and dusted my pants. The joke would be on him. I wanted to go get my camera. He took the hint and stood, adjusting the front of his pants to obscure the bulge that had formed again. If he had led me to believe that I was teaching an alien how to kiss, he could walk uncomfortably for a few meters.

"Take me to my ship, sir!" I said with a smile. It was his turn to shake his head.

"See! You're getting it," I laughed, and patted his arm, if only just to touch him again.

It was a good day, and that wasn't even counting that I had gotten a job!

Chapter Eleven
Her Job

Drex

Exploring Katy's mouth with my own was much more than I had expected for this day. I'd just wanted to provide her some comfort in a world that might not feel like her own. I told myself I cared because I was a good host. That it was my job; but it felt like something more. I wanted her to feel safe and happy. Each smile made me want the next.

When she questioned if I knew what kissing was, I was surprised. Was I so bad that she thought it might not exist on Xavia? Maybe I was a little rusty. Maybe there were some cultural differences in our kisses. Maybe I was just a bit nervous. Truly, I was nervous. But I couldn't miss the opportunity to feign cluelessness. A little humor in what had been trying times so far.

Her mouth had been cool, wet, and soft. Her body tensed as my tongues gently explored her. She may not had known I had individual control of them until that moment. As much as I enjoyed the kiss, forbidden thoughts invaded about other soft interiors and sets of lips. I brought my attention back to her mouth, but it was too late. I was already growing strong down there. I didn't want to make her feel uncomfortable, so I regretfully backed away to compose myself. As much as I respected her safety and comfort, my body betrayed its growing desire for her.

I was glad she was happy to see her sister, even though we hadn't stayed long. That confused me a bit. I thought she would want to be with her for much longer, but she seemed content to have laid eyes on her. Maybe she was uncomfortable seeing her sister so demonstratively affectionate with her host. Was it because they had just met, and she thought they should have more decorum? Or was it because he was an alien? Being open to meeting new cultures didn't necessarily mean she thought species should intermix. I didn't get that impression from her, though. Perhaps it was less about "aliens" and more about the lies that had brought her here. It made me angry at depths reserved for the Orkain, that humans would uproot their own by deception and dump them. I wanted to keep her safe from them as much as I did from the Orkain. If I had my way, neither Orkain nor US government would ever lay eyes on her again. I didn't want any harm to come to Katy.

"This is one of my favorite trails," I admitted as we walked along the water. What I didn't admit was that it was amazing to see her beautiful form walking it. She was making everything I enjoyed, better.

"I can see why. It's wonderful." She smiled at me, and I nodded, but all I could think about was that *she* was wonderfully gorgeous; the scenery quickly fading. I wanted those soft pink lips engulfed in mine again.

The trail took us away from the ship, but not too far. Katy appeared relatively fit for her kind. She kept up with my long strides despite our height difference. She didn't seem bothered at all by the speed, and so I relaxed into the walk. I would need to be alert to keep her safe in these woods. There had been no sightings of the Orkain today, but they could come out to hunt at any time. They seemed intelligent enough to change up their routines. They were, unfortunately, good hunters.

Eventually, we had to cut away from the stream and climb a hill to where the ship's pod had landed. If I expected Katy to be excited, she wasn't exactly. There, I had a guard, Lian. Lian was one of our younger adult males. He had just barely missed the cut to be a host. While he was an eligible bachelor, it was better he had some time to mature, develop his career, and establish himself more before hosting. He had a lot of potential. I had hoped he'd be able to host one of the women from the next set of guests. I couldn't quite see the programing continuing at this point. We'd require the US government to be honest with its people. We couldn't accept another group of women told falsehoods.

Lian visibly tensed when he saw us. He gave me a small bow of his head, and a deeper bow to Katy. Katy returned the bow.

"Katy, this is Lian. Lian, Katy."

"Kay-tee," he said, "Pleased to meet you."

Lian sounded good, but I knew that was probably the majority of his English, just a few phrases we had learned. Once he learned he had not been picked, he hadn't taken the opportunity to learn more, saying he'd learn it by the next round of women. That had sort of cemented my thoughts that Lian needed more time to mature. He was still choosing *easy* over his future. He would learn in time.

That's partly why I had him guarding the ship, he would be able to meet all the women and maybe he'd take the initiative to learn more so he could be a good host in the future.

Katy held out her hand, and Lian looked confused. I told him in our language that he was supposed to shake it. It was a custom he should have already learned. He looked too happy touching her. I was happy when he stopped.

As if Lian knew he'd gotten too much enjoyment from it, he gave me a quick glance of apology. I gave him a stern look but let it pass. He hadn't done anything wrong. It would have been rude not to shake her hand. I couldn't help but feel possessive.

"Anything to report?" I asked.

"No one inside. No sightings from anyone this morning." Lian stepped to the side so that we could enter the ship.

I stepped into the hallway with her, more curious than anything else. I trusted Lian had checked all the rooms.

"The one over there is mine, I think. Oh yes, there's my name," she pointed to a small placard signage. I waited in the hallway to give her some privacy.

I could see how she could get confused, the rooms all looked the same. She'd have to teach me to read English. We had learned the language mostly orally. My written language skills were lacking. I knew how some of the letters looked, but it seemed the same symbol was used for multiple sounds, and I didn't know how to go about writing them either.

When I heard her squeal, I rushed into the room, took a fighting stance, and scanned the room for dangers—starting with the ceiling, thinking about the ugly winged body of an Orkain. The ceiling was just a ceiling, and when I saw Katy, she hefted a black object in her hand.

"My camera! It survived the trip," she said before registering my reaction. "Oh, I'm sorry. I'm not in any danger. No one in here but me."

"It's okay. I'm sorry. I'm on edge. I don't want anything to happen to you."

She nodded resolutely. I went to step out of the room again. "You can stay if you like," she said.

It was my turn to nod, and I took that as permission to look around the room, instead of just scanning it for dangers. The largest strange device was the stasis-pod, a human-sized tube leaning against the wall, attached to smaller tubes and wires.

"Is that where you slept? We got your bed way wrong."

"Yes…no…" she changed her answer when she realized what I meant. "They put us into a deep stasis. It wasn't really sleep," she explained.

"What was it?"

"I could tell time had passed when I woke up, but I guess it was like a dreamless passing of time. It felt like a long nap."

"That doesn't sound too bad."

"No, the people that developed those things seemed to have done a good job. I dunno, I guess we will find out if there's any lasting effects, and if it's the same going back."

It hurt me to hear her talk about leaving. While she took it as the next sequential event, I had trouble thinking about any sort of life without her. Not just the hope she brought my people, but the hope and cheer she provided me personally. Katy was a bright light.

Katy packed things from her drawers into a couple of larger bags. She had some clothing, and bottles of different things. I tried not to pry even though I had a lot of questions. She took all the grooming items beside the stasis pod, and I wondered what she had looked like before going into the stasis pod. Was her hair this long? Did she like it shorter? I liked the way her hair was now. I imagined caressing her neck under her flowy tresses.

Soon she had two full bags and was closing them. I put one on each shoulder despite her protesting that she could carry one. She would do no such thing. I was happy to care for her in any possible way. Plus, doing something physical helped take my mind off other things. She kept her camera close with a strap securing it over her neck so that it was within arm's reach. It lay across her wonderful breasts which were evident despite wearing the loose tunics she had been choosing.

I must have been staring too long, because she said, "Honestly, I packed the bras, but I don't think I'm going to wear them. Why set up that precedent here?"

"What is a bras?" I asked.

She laughed, and said, "Maybe I'll show you sometime. They're to secure the breasts so they don't move around so much."

"Why would you want to do that?"

"I guess it's uncomfortable for some people, but the contraption is pretty uncomfortable too."

I shrugged. I couldn't imagine something securing the breasts would be very sexy, but I also hadn't seen anything Katy wear not become something sexy. All fabrics managed to drape over her body pleasingly.

"Let's get on home," she said.

I liked that she had called it home. She hadn't called it 'her' home or 'our' home, but it was better than nothing. I couldn't wait to get her home. I wanted an excuse to be close to her, in private, even if we weren't going to do anything. I wanted her all to myself.

We said goodbye to Lian. I noticed Katy didn't offer her hand again. She kept distance from him. I wasn't mad about that. In fact, I was quite pleased. Lian needed to learn a little respect.

Chapter Twelve
Have Some Fun

Katy

I was happy to get my stuff, but Lian sort of gave me the creeps. I knew they didn't have many females here, but he could have at least shown respect in front of his prince and his prince's guest. He looked me up and down like I was a snack. If he could, he would have grabbed me and flown off with me, like the Orkain he guarded me from Maybe after seeing more of our kind, he'd chill. It didn't matter. I was just glad that I didn't have to deal with him. I was glad Drex was my host.

The Xavian men were handsome, so I had chalked up my attraction to Drex to his good looks, but I was quickly gaining a preference for him. I loved his well-defined, broad shoulders. I loved his smile. I ached to touch his horns and explore him with my hands. When we made out, the heat and scent radiating from him were intoxicating. I looked forward to being in the privacy of his home.

I tried to rationalize all the things I wanted to do with Drex. My mind went in all directions. I wondered what he physically looked like. Surely, he had some sort of penis. I had felt the bulge, and the United States of America wouldn't have gone through all this trouble if they didn't think mating was possible. Another part of me considered the political ramifications. Wasn't this exactly what the government wanted? Screw them. They weren't even here. I might as well have some fun before going back. That was my point being here, right? To explore a new planet and culture and then return to Earth in a much better financial state. What better way to explore, than to *explore?*

It took less time to get back than I expected, and suddenly we were alone in his house. I guess we had taken a longer way to see my sister and the creek. I hadn't even asked to go back that way with my camera. I had completely forgotten. My mind had definitely been elsewhere. He had seemed pretty determined to get us home, too. He carried my bags to my room and set them down at the foot of the bed.

Grateful, I approached him for another hug, but my hands found other ideas. His pectoral muscles tightened underneath my fingers. He was puffing up for me. There wasn't any need; he was very firm. I craned my neck to bring my lips toward his. Our lips hardly touched before his mouth was open and his tongue pressed against my lips.

This time his tongues were much more forceful. They explored my mouth greedily. They ran along my teeth and wrapped around my own tongue. I could feel his need to explore me, and I wanted to be explored. He wanted me bad. And I was getting so turned on. Every swipe of his tongue shot electricity through my body and core. My arms moved frantically to his shoulders, desperate to pull him tight against my body. My leg drew up and reached around his waist. His fingers dug into my thighs as he hoisted me over his growing need. I wrapped my legs around him as best I could as we made out. My hands combed through his hair. It was thick and course. I didn't touch his horns, but I wanted to. Boy, did I want to.

The delicate fabric of the linen pants I wore couldn't disguise how wet I was getting. I gave a couple of soft thrusts over top of him. His mouth pressed harder against mine.

He carried me with ease over to the side of the bed and laid me gently on my back. His mouth moved to my neck and his tongues drew swirls on my sensitive skin. Goosebumps and tingles traveled my arms. He supported himself over me with an arm on either side of me. His intense gaze drew my focus before his eyes roved my body. I melted under his watch. I only wanted his touch.

Then he was no longer on the bed with me. He crouched beside me, and with a yank of my ankles, had his head between my legs. His hands dragged along my inner thighs. He could see how wet I was from his vantage point. He met my eyes again while a finger played along my waistband, asking for permission. And if I wondered his intentions, he licked his top lip with two of his tongues.

God. My channel twitched tight against itself, and I knew I wouldn't be able to say no. I needed to know what those tongues felt like on my skin, and inside me. I nodded as my own hands fumbled toward my waist, signaling my growing needs. His broad hands made short work of my pants and underwear, pulling them down to my ankles. He took my shoes off one at a time, while my pussy flashed on full display.

While I worried the walk had warmed me up, his hands crept up my calves, grabbed my knees, and pulled me wide. His horns grazed my thighs. With his head between my legs, he took me in. It made me dizzy with desire. He moaned close to my mound. His hot breath sent fire up my spine, arching it toward him. His nose nuzzled the curls, and whether he knew it, he breathed warm on my clit. My own breath caught in my throat. He nosed me, brushing against my clit. Moving my hair for a better look, he discovered my clit. His eyes glued to my face; he gave it the slightest flick with his tongue. Gauging the positive reaction, he nuzzled it gently with his nose before dragging his tongue across it. Holy hell.

"Oh, that feels so good," I encouraged softly.

He moved his tongue back and forth, alternating between writing with its tip and wide swipes with its broadness. Drex's horns pressed against my thighs. The combination of the softness of his tongue and the hardness of his horns was so hot, and he was working my clit, swirling his tongue over it.

I was getting close. I pressed close to him as I began panting. Then his tongues separated, one on my clit and one on either side of my slick pussy, wringing the pleasure from it. They dragged slowly upward until they hemmed in my clit—all three tips playing on the bundle of nerves.

He was sending me into a frenzy. I bucked against his face, urging him to keep going. I grabbed his horns. They were hard and strange and so freaking hot. I steered him into my pussy. My body convulsed as pleasure pulsed deep inside me like waves. With the smash of his tongues in a final crest, my body pulled tight, every muscle contracting, before I collapsed back onto the bed, my upper body and head falling to the mattress from where they'd lifted.

"Oh my gosh," I whispered. Holy heck that was good. I panted lightly, trying to catch my breath.

He didn't move from between my legs. He looked up at me wickedly, thoroughly pleased with himself. I traced indentions on his horns with my hand as I tried to take stock of my body. He licked me off of his lips and wiped his chin. He came up from between my legs, staying close.

"Thanks," I said breathlessly, still not giving much thought to anything above my waist. His cock pulsed against my leg.

He smiled. "My pleasure."

He gave me a damp kiss on my nose, and after another intimate moment where we shared the same breathing space, he gracefully got off of me, pivoted me fully onto the bed, and left me in privacy to fall into a soft, enjoyable sleep. I dreamed.

Chapter Thirteen
Rotha

Drex

It had been a dream come true, laying Katy down on the soft bed, her hair scattered around her like the rays of the sun. I ran my breath down her body, and teased the edges of her clothing as I asked permission. She bit her lip and nodded forcefully, almost racing me to get her pants off first. I almost passed out with desire as I spread her legs for my feast.

The Earth government had given us some anatomical illustrations in our provided education, but she was different from those. She had the most delectable tuft of hair which kept her scent close to her body. I rubbed the curls with my nose and took in her intoxicating scent. She had soft folds which I knew were hiding her entrance. What was the same was a curious little bump, a peak above her entrance, with a little hood. I breathed on it and received a reaction. It was apparently quite sensitive. Small touches caused her thighs to clench the sides of my face. Pressure on my horns sent fantastic sensation through my skull. I lapped at the button and received the most beautiful moans from her mouth as I felt my chin wet with her juices. With her encouragement, I kept it up. My cock spasmed repeatedly against the mattress, seeking to be part of the action, desiring to be a part of her. Finally, she gripped my horns like I ached for her to do, taking control of my head, pressing her mound into me, her back coming off the bed. I kept a firm grip with my mouth and moved my tongues to explore her exterior. That did it, she was coming undone, and I hadn't even entered her. My center tongue pressed against her button, and the other two came up and put pressure on the sides. Katy's entire body clenched and held me as she screamed in ecstasy, her hands squeezing my horns. I kept pressure as her entire core shivered until she crumpled onto the bed.

I breathed small kisses on her damp skin, resting my head against her, and reveled in the smells and tastes of what I'd just accomplished. My cock throbbed, but I was otherwise satiated by her sex and intense release.

I pulled myself up and got close so that we were face to face. Looking into her small, unfocused eyes and that dopey smile, she was happily spent, relishing in the glow. It thrilled me to see her finally relaxed and feeling safe. I was so proud of what I had done, and I would gladly do it a million times more.

Then, I felt it.

It was a giant jerk behind my heart, like it was being grabbed and pulled deeper into my body. I jolted. I played it off like I was adjusting myself, unsure if Katy noticed. It was surprising, painful, like an involuntary spasm. I needed to leave and compose myself. I took the corner of the blanket that she wasn't lying on and pulled it up over her. I took a pillow and put it under her head. She was already beginning to fall asleep as I made my leave.

On the other side of the door, in the safety of the hall, I had a chance to consider what had happened. I no longer felt it. I didn't have a heart injury or anything like that. It had been so quick; I easily dismissed it. But before I did, I considered what it *could* be. My father had explained that it had been a tender pull on his soul whenever he was near my mother. He had explained that it wasn't just nervousness or excitement, but it was a physical sensation that was the start of rotha. While I respected—probably idolized—my parents' relationship, I hadn't asked much about it. Now I wished my father was here, so he could tell me more.

Were there other biological symptoms I might experience? What was the timeline on this thing?

I racked my brain for any memories of their rotha. I remembered that my parents always seemed to know where the other was. Even in a crowd, or having just entered a building, they easily found each other. That wasn't helpful to me now, though. I knew where Katy was. She was just in the other room.

I didn't even know if rotha was possible with someone outside of our species. She was from an entirely different world. And I had never felt it before, obviously. I wouldn't know for sure. Perhaps it was pent-up sexual excitement, or like a heart defect. I dreaded feeling it again, but I was also curious. What had it been? Remembering my parents' party trick wasn't helpful. What I needed to know was if this was real, and if it was going to affect her too. I doubted it. She wasn't of my species. She already had a human rotha tie, the man she was supposed to marry on Earth. The planet where she was returning. I'd never been one to hope for a defective heart, but at this point, it seemed better than a broken heart that rotha would dictate when she fled Xavia.

Chapter Fourteen
Telefunctional

Katy

My eyes blinked open as I woke up. My head had sunk deep into the pillow, muffling any possible noises that might have disturbed me. The light in the room was soft. I wasn't sure what time it was, and the shades made it difficult to know, but it seemed to be evening. I had fallen asleep for a couple of hours, and it had been peaceful, enjoyable, even. My body felt incredibly relaxed, and then I remembered why. Drex had dived between my legs, ravished me with his three tongues, sent me into ecstasy, then wrapped me in warmth and the best sleep I'd had since arriving on Xavia.

My eyes felt heavy, contented. I wasn't sure where he had gone. It seemed he had left rather abruptly but my mind was a little blurry on those details between the edges of orgasm and basically passing out. My body hadn't experienced such highs and contentment in…well, not that intensely in forever. Was it the adrenaline, the forbidden-ness, the alien-ness?…just all of it. I wasn't about to believe that there was a real connection. Maybe some chemistry. Okay, definitely some good chemistry. And some skill. He'd been tentative and gentle. I didn't know if that was technique or a shallow learning curve. I still had no knowledge of what females Xavians looked like down there, if we were similar. I didn't even know what *he* looked like down there.

I guessed it was time for me to get up and make an appearance, so he didn't think he'd inadvertently killed me. Death by orgasm. That would be one for the History of Humans on this planet. I untucked my pants-less legs. My pants were not strewn on the ground where they'd been discarded earlier. Instead, they had been folded and placed on the edge of the bed. I recognized the tucks. All the clothes provided me had been folded by him. I appreciated his attention to detail. I was sorry he didn't have someone who might stay with him permanently. He would probably make someone happy, but that wasn't why I was here. My stay would be temporary.

I slipped on the pants to dash across the hall and clean up a bit more. I brought my brush with me, because one touch to the back of my head disclosed a positive rat's nest. I hoped he wouldn't catch a glimpse of me before I cleaned up. He had seemed proud he had made me cum like that, and I was proud of it too, but I didn't want him getting a big head by seeing what sort of mess I was still in hours later. I quietly opened my door and took big leaping tiptoe steps to the bathroom.

After rinsing off in the shower, I got into the plunge pool. I couldn't help it. It felt like continuation of, well, a nice evening. The water smelled like lavender and I couldn't help but wonder if Drex had taken a soak too, or if he'd adjusted it in case I wanted to take a dip. A fresh towel folded by the pool told me it was the latter. He was definitely a good host.

I dried off, slipped on my clothes again, and after towel-drying and combing my hair, I made my appearance in the main living area.

"I made you food but let me warm it up. I was expecting you a bit sooner," Drex said with his eyebrows raised.

"I guess I was more tired than I thought."

"Or perhaps I did an OK job?" he offered. It was partly a joke, but his look of earnest didn't escape me. He wanted to know.

"You did a great job," I said. "I think I even said 'thank you.'"

"Yeah, I thought was a little weird. Is it weird?"

"I dunno. Is it?"

We both laughed, and I suddenly wanted to be close to him again. I had had a good time, but I was still sort of shy. In my defense, I'd never been in this situation before, living with someone that I had just met who was very, very attractive. Perhaps these next months wouldn't be as awful as I imagined they would be.

He put my food into the oven and poured me a glass of purple-colored liquid.

"Is this alcohol?" I asked, giving it a sniff. It definitely smelled like alcohol, maybe wine.

"I don't know the word 'alcohol.' It has some enjoyable, mind-altering effects. We call it fage."

"Sounds like alcohol. We ferment beverages with sugar and when you drink it, it temporarily changes your mood and reaction times. If you drink a lot of it, it makes you sick."

"Your culture seems really focused on sugar. It's from the fah plant. It goes through an aging process. It makes people giddy or euphoric. I think you'll like it."

I gave it a cautionary sip. He was right. It didn't taste sweet. It had an almost vinegary tang to it, but it wasn't unpleasant. I took another sip.

He poured himself a glass too and sat beside me, crossing an ankle over a knee.

"Is that like a TV too, can you watch shows or movies?" I asked about the smaller settit in the room.

"Like the educational ones your government showed us?" he asked, a little surprised that I'd want to watch such things.

"Um, no, maybe something more entertaining and fun. Does it do that?"

"Not really, these are for communication. We watched your government's media on them, but we only record for basic communication."

"No movies? No TV shows? Nobody films people pretending to be other people for others' entertainment?" We were so technologically similar, it rocked me when something ended up being so different.

He looked amused but he shook his head. "Not really, I saw some of those re-enactments in your media, like that?"

I couldn't imagine any government-sponsored re-enactments being entertaining, nothing like the mountain of good media we had created. It was the sort of thing that made us…Earthlings, I guessed.

"Well, lucky for you, I brought some!" I said as I handed him my glass of fage and basically ran to my room. I returned with my laptop which had a huge library of media. "Did you say you were able to watch the government stuff on your device?" It now made sense why the settit was in portrait. It was for communication between their tall people, not necessarily for watching trash-TV.

"I can take it to Davian. He does technical conversion stuff," he said.

"No, that's fine. Maybe later. We can watch on this. It's just a small screen." I set it on the coffee table—fah table?—and pulled it close. "You are about to learn so-o much about Earth, stuff you probably don't want to know. It'll be like a crash-course, or a car crash…one or the other, y'know"

He didn't know, but he stretched his arm wide to accept me close to him. I wrapped limbs around him. He was warm. I didn't even need a blanket.

I clicked a few buttons and explained the format and the premise of my favorite show, *Telefunctional*, a mockumentary set in a call center. I knew some things wouldn't translate, but I decided that was going to be the fun of it. We had to start somewhere, right?

I had to pause and explain a lot of things to Drex, but he seemed to enjoy learning about my culture. It was nice to reverse things and have him asking the questions. Although, the United States government probably would have wanted me to teach him more useful things.

It became more difficult to explain things as the fage kicked in. It was a mild, sort-of dopey happiness melting me from the top of my head down—a pleasant light-headedness. I giggled. Drex had finished his glass but he didn't seem to be as affected. He was much larger than me, and had built up tolerance, having drunk it previously, I supposed. Maybe he shouldn't have given me as much as he had poured himself.

"Maybe I shouldn't have given you a full glass," he said as if hearing my thoughts. I must have looked drowsy. "How are you feeling?"

"Pretty dang good," I said. I had lost track of where in the show we were, and instead had my head nestled into his chest. He reached for the half-empty glass in my hand, but it only renewed my interest in it. I sat up to take another sip. The flavor was growing on me as it warmed, and as I warmed. "Do people ever heat this up and serve it?" I asked.

"They do, like fah. We can try it that way…next time," he said strategically. I took one more sip before he stole the glass away, placing it across him on the table. I was fine with that, happy even. I slipped an arm behind his back as we cuddled. It felt right. I didn't feel like I was in foreign country with a stranger. I was with Drex, and we were watching my favorite show on a comfy couch…or urish, as he called it. With the sounds of my favorite show soothing my soul, I soon drifted off to sleep tucked against him.

Eventually, Drex moved out from underneath me. I was no longer asleep, but I pretended to be. I wanted to see what he would do. He closed the laptop which I realized was two or three shows past from when I remember falling asleep. He had sat there and watched it while I slept. He put his arms underneath me and easily scooped me up. He softly pressed me to his body. I wished for a moment he'd take me to his bed, but he did no such thing. The man was painfully respectful. He took me down the hall to my room, where he tucked me under the covers and fluffed my pillow underneath my head.

He put a hand to my face and caressed my cheek as I felt his weight release on the bed. I wasn't ready for him to go. I grabbed his hand, inviting him to stay with me. He moved closer and contorted to take off his shirt, so I let him do so. He climbed into bed with me and wrapped his strong arms around me. I wanted him there with me. Before I could relish how our bodies meshed together, I was already falling back asleep, safe in his arms.

Chapter Fifteen
Visiting Town

Katy

Drex wasn't in bed when I woke, but his scent was still on the sheets. I was also firmly tucked into the covers; I assumed that was his doing. I smelled food cooking in the kitchen. He didn't seem to need as much sleep as I did. I didn't know if that was an alien-thing, or a Drex-thing. I felt I had been sleeping a lot. Maybe I just needed more to recover from all the space travel. It was nice though. I finally felt like I was getting good sleep, which was a struggle on Earth.

I adjusted the soft pillow and spotted my camera on the nightstand. All ideas of falling back asleep flew out the window. I sat up, held it, and realized for the first time in a long time, I felt excited to be holding it. I didn't know if that'd ever be the case again. My job had brought me so much pain and kept open so many wounds I thought would never heal, but here, it was different. I could set all of that aside and take photographs of the lives going on here, and I was happily separate from it, an observer without my own story about failed weddings, tear drops on a wedding dress, or returned gifts. I would be taking photos of different things for different reasons, no longer tied down with all that pain, all that debt, and all that insecurity. It felt freeing.

I jumped out of bed, excited for the day. I started with breakfast, taking photos of the process of fah. Drex was a sport and let me take photos of him enjoying a hot mug of it. Then, I took photos of the exterior of his home. I had made him promise to take me into the town today to take photos of their abandoned homes. Those were important, too. Part of who they were now was based on who they were just a generation ago. Drex told me he would take me anywhere I wanted, possibly because he knew I'd go there without him, otherwise. And yes, if I thought he wouldn't take me, I'd totally go by myself. So I was glad we just agreed to go together.

Signs for roads and stores met us. Signage wasn't a foreign concept to them; it just hadn't carried to their new homes in the emergency. There had been generations of technology before then. I snapped photo after photo before we even reached what was the edge of the town.

"This was Frustnerrd. The outskirts of it, at least." He pointed out the splattering of buildings which looked like any abandoned, industrial part of town, but the rest of the town would be abandoned too. "We used a lot of concrete which retained heat."

"Wouldn't it make it more difficult to find people in a concrete town?" Referring to the Orkain.

"You'd think, but there wasn't anywhere to hide either."

I nodded. I thought about our sprawling parking lots and sidewalks with small immature trees planted every specific number of yards. There wouldn't be anywhere to hide if you were on foot.

"Did you have vehicles?"

"Like personal vehicles? No. We had mass transit."

Some parts of Earth had gone to mass transit, but we still had a lot of personal vehicles. They were part of the mass transit system, could be put on trains, or attached as convoys to go longer distances, but humans still loved being able to go fast to individual places. Something like that might be good for a place like this. It could act as personal armor…until you had to get out of the car.

"Did you live in this town?" I asked, which was really my way of asking if his family ruled over it.

"Nearby. My father had to push so hard to get people to evacuate. It was difficult for people to understand they were safer in the jungle in makeshift homes rather than in town. We lost so many people."

"That must have been hard for your father."

"It was. Thankfully the people who survived did not blame him. Only our most adaptable people survived."

I had noticed that. It was a lot of young men who could and were willing to survive on little. There were few young and old.

A distant squeal startled me. Drex put an arm around me and even in that moment, I realized why he had been so close. He was protecting me. He opened a door to an old store and led me inside.

"All of the buildings are unlocked for this very reason," he said. His eyes cut upward through the heavy glass door.

"Was that an——?" I didn't even want to finish my question. An Orkain.

He nodded. "We should be safe in here. It hasn't seen us. It's just nearby."

I climbed into the store window to catch sight of it, my camera in hand.

"What are you doing?"

"I need to photograph them, too. Your lives are centered around them."

"Please get down." He said it calmly but he looked ready to physically remove me from the window. There wasn't any danger. Still, his worry touched me. So, I offered my hand, and he helped me down. I was then able to look around the store, which was some sort of general store. I saw lots of goods, specialty food. I recognized the soaff in Drex's shower.

"Most supplies were delivered. Stores like these were if you needed something last minute."

It was like going to a foreign store—fun to look around even if I wasn't sure what it all was. I didn't notice a lot of branding. There were choices and options, but nothing seemed to be vying for your attention more than anything else. It was just sort of 'buy what works best for you' rather than the commercialism of Earth. It made things sort of boring, but I also felt a lot less stimulated.

"We had two general stores like this… another on the other side of town, for convenience's sake, but they carried the same thing."

I wasn't about to tell him how we had hundreds of stores like this all selling sort of the same but different stuff, and that they were all different companies. It seemed pretty silly.

"What about the rest of these stores then?" There were plenty of store fronts.

"Those are specialty stores. People sell their handmade goods there, art, and creative takes on different functional pieces, like furniture, or food."

"Like small businesses?" I asked. I thought about some of the boutiques.

"Yes, very small, just what wares they want to sell."

"I'd love to snap some photos in a couple of those too," I said. I liked looking at people's art. It would be interesting to see how their art differed pre- and post-alien invasion.

Despite the huge drop in population, it seemed that their condition of living hadn't changed too dramatically. Their planet was relatively small and their population was much smaller than Earth's even before their social collapse.

"Did my government offer to help you get rid of the Orkain?" I asked.

"They did. They tried, but they weren't able to find the homebase as they called it of the Orkain. They just keep coming back. Earth doesn't have any sort of planetary defense for us."

I wondered if the US would even help them if they could. They preferred doing business with people who were already at a disadvantage, present company included.

"What do you use the holmium for?" asked Drex.

"It's used in our technology. It's in my camera. It's in that stasis pod I was in. It's in all of our vehicles. We use it everywhere."

"And Earth is out of it?"

"It never had much of it. We call it a rare Earth metal. We're not even good at reclaiming it from our trash. We haven't found any good substitute for it. I don't know much about, but I guess I'm a part of the use-cycle. I mean, even before I was a tradeable property."

"You are not and never will you be property, Katy," he said firmly as he finally decided we could move next door.

This one had lots of beautiful tapestries.

"One person made all these?"

"No, I believe this was a group. However, one of the women, Gulshan, is teaching a new group…" he trailed off. Tragedy was everywhere.

I fingered the coarse braids intricately folded. This couldn't be lost. I took photos.

"Would you like one for your room?" Drex asked, holding up a rug much longer than he was.

"Oh no, I couldn't," I said.

"I will pay her. I will also bring her back some to dismantle make into more functional pieces, too."

I brushed my fingers across one that was much softer. "Maybe a small one," I said. The colors faded from dark red to the faintest orange. It would be handsome next to my bed.

He rolled up it up and tucked it under his arm. "I hope your room is OK," he said, another worried look in his eyes.

"It's wonderful. You've been an excellent host. Maybe the best I've ever had," I laughed, but it was true. No one had ever gone through such care to make sure that I felt safe and at home. And the physical comfort was no joke either.

Drex sported a proud grin as he rolled up a couple more pieces while I snapped photos.

"Will you introduce me to Gulshan?" I asked. "I'd love to take photos of her and her process. Maybe during one of her classes."

"That sounds perfect," said Drex.

I brushed my hand against his. I was enjoying our outing even if he seemed a bit on edge. It was difficult to feel uncomfortable when he was so close and keeping watch.

He took me into several other stores with pottery, wall art, and the like. I appreciated the small town feel to a place that had industry. I wondered how America had missed out on such a combination. We tried, but we also loved convenience. I still had so many questions about their history, but I know it hurt him to discuss it. I hadn't seen Drex use anything like currency yet. It was something to ask later.

I was so entranced by all the art. It was good to see something outside his walls and the backdrop of the (albeit beautiful) jungle. And I think Drex enjoyed showing it all to me too. He had a big smile on his face whenever he looked over at me, enjoying the items of his world. I couldn't help but smile back.

Between stores, he pulled me into what looked like an alley, but its center had a tiny pavilion, perhaps the back of a restaurant. Low-slung lights were strung across the space, and a fountain still bubbled in the center. Somehow, it felt like we weren't supposed to be there. I imagined that we had just escaped the eyes of onlookers. He pressed me up against a cool pillar and kissed me passionately. I was enthralled. His kisses were intense, foreign, and breathtaking. He pulled away too soon.

The whole thing was way too romantic, especially when the glow bugs came out in early evening as we made our way back to Drex's home. I couldn't dismiss the ambiance, like I was walking among the stars. It had been in the midst of stars that I found Drex. And here we were, walking together. He was tall, stoic, and had spent the entire day humoring my desire to take photos of everything. It had been a delight. If anything, I would be going back to Earth with some good memories.

I was thankful for Drex, and as soon as he closed the door to his home with me inside, I wanted to show him just how thankful. I wanted to touch him again. He had hardly put down the things from our travels when I approached him with what I hoped was a sexy look in my eye, my hand grazed his chest.

"Would you like to get in the pool with me?" I asked.

He looked surprised but he quickly stumbled over the word "*yes*" and his own feet, as if I'd change my mind if he was too slow to answer. I took him by the hand and led him to the bathing room. I danced around, planning to strip for him. I wasn't usually big on that sort of thing. I didn't like so much attention or focus on my body. But, here, with Drex, it was different. I could tell Drex craved me. I was exotic, and he didn't have any other humans to compare me to. That was surprisingly liberating. He liked me, a lot. That was evident with the bulge in his pants that was already growing.

I wrapped my arms around my tunic and pulled tight on it so that it raised my breasts toward my chin as I took off the shirt. My breasts bounced down into view. Drex stood by the door, stunned. He made a small groan of a noise as I ran my hands along my collar bone, down my cleavage, and underneath my round breasts. My pink nipples stood erect, exposed to the air and the excitement.

I played with the waist of my pants as I walked toward the shower, my back to Drex. I heard his footsteps as he padded behind me. I pulled my waistband down in the back so he could get a peek of my ass. He cursed under his breath in admiration. I bent down and pulled down my pants with a quick motion, my full ass in his view. He had drawn close to me now. I felt his hand on my bare waist, a thumb daring to graze the curve of it. He was watching his hand interacting with my ass in full admiration. I stepped into the shower and pressed the buttons I had settled on as a wonderful shower. Water came from all angles and splashed my body. I pressed my back against the cool shower wall and ran my hands along my breasts, down my belly, and brushed my inner thighs before moving back up to my massage my breasts in the warm water.

Drex still wasn't moving much on his own, shy, maybe. I pulled him into the shower, fully clothed. He didn't seem to mind. He closed some the distance between us. The wet linen showed the outlines of the vast, rippled muscles on his chest; it clung to his six pack of abdominals and his obliques. Muscles long and tight dove at a sharp angle to his crotch. His pants were wet too. His cock created a shelf to collect water.

I lightly touched his cock through his pants as I reached up and ran my hands along his wet shirt. His hand returned to my waist. I could tell he was eager to touch me, but let me take the lead. I played with the waistband of his pants. His dick jumped with my proximity. I grabbed his shirt ends instead and peeled the fabric from his luscious, turquoise skin. He glimmered in the water. I let the shirt slop to the floor with a wet noise. I pressed my chest against his abs, my breasts ballooned upward with the pressure and we both admired the water fall from all sides of my breasts before he nudged my head upward and swept me into a slow, long passionate kiss. His tongues held together and softly probed along my lips and danced with my own tongue. Rhythmically, his cock pressed into my belly with his kiss.

I wrenched my hands away from stroking his wonderful chest and shoulders to let them fall lower to his waistband. I played with the buttons that typically held his pants on, but even without them, his pants would not be able to overcome the tautness created by his massive cock to fall down. I was excited to see him, but I was also nervous. What would it look like? It seemed huge, and I didn't know how comfortable it would be. Would I be turned on?

His hands were on my back, his fingers dragged down my ass, running his hands along the shelf of my ass. It tickled, but I loved how much he was teasing me with his hands. I popped the top button on his pants, and he grunted. He grabbed my ass cheeks, hoisting me up easily just to sit me on the slate bench. The water faucets keeping my body warm, he got down on his knees. Grabbing my legs, he pulled me close to the edge, and there he nibbled at my thighs, getting tantalizing close to my swelling sex. The anticipation was too much. I put my hands on his horns and pressed him inward toward my entrance. His lips enveloped my mound and the soft pressure and gentle sucking pulled juices from my body.

He put his top lip on my clit and kept steady pressure as his still entwined tongue explored the edges of my entrance, working its way in deep wide circles through my folds. He licked my slit. I let out a small cry of pleasure as his tongue slipped inside and up. My body pulsed with each swipe of his tongue. He made a doubtful noise, and I answered by grabbing his horns tighter and pushing him closer. My juices mixed with the shower water dripping down my folds and puddled on the bench.

While keeping steady pressure on my clit with his upper lip, he pressed his tongue into me again. This time slightly farther, waiting out the tiny, involuntary buck of my body. His tongue slipped deeper. I clenched the thickest part of his tongue. And as he pulled it out, he separated and dragged each length along the edges of my entrance. Every stroke of pressure on my G-spot rewarded him a crash of my hips and a tight convulsion of my channel. Each upward curled stroke of his tongue braced my clit from the interior as he pressed his lip against the outside. The crescendo built as his tongues reached deep. My core tightened; I orgasmed into his mouth. My juices poured over his tongues, his reward for the pleasure he'd provided me. I lost the edges of time and space in the waves.

I sat almost slumped, trying to catch my breath as he caressed my folds, triangle, and inner thighs with the soft touch of his breath and lips. He licked the juices off his bottom lip with that amazing tongue that made me feel such intensity, in triplicate. I recovered quickly. He had distracted me long enough.

I wanted to know.

I needed to know.

What were under those pants?

As much as it pained me to move him from his place between my legs, I pulled on his arms so that he knew I wanted him to stand. He was now soaked, head to toe, the shower blasting him as his tongue blasted through me. I wrestled the buttons on his pants which were just off to the side. The fabric folded over in a triangle, and when I finished the last button, his uncovered, bare cock popped out and almost smacked me in the face. If I hadn't been sitting, I would have fallen. I plastered myself against the shower wall, away from...the freaking *creature*. I don't know what I expected, besides a monstrously large cock. I didn't expect two more.

Like his tongue.

There were three.

"Is it OK?" he asked, as if it might not be enough!

It would have been funny if I wasn't so nervous. After a moment, he realized my reaction was not one of pity, but of kinky panic. He stepped back to give me some space, so that I might not feel trapped. I hoped he hadn't seen the anxiety in my eyes.

It was erect, pointing at me, like it had chosen me for a very special mission. I wasn't sure if I was up for it. I mean, it might be fine for the female of his species, but at this point, I was just trying to wrap my mind around it.

The three wrapped around themselves just like his tongue did to make a thick trunk. The middle one was the longest with the largest head; the other two were much shorter, and would perhaps be acceptable, if there had been one of them, instead of two being overshadowed by the third.

Drex stayed quiet, flexing his specimen slowly for my approval. He moved them around each other, in what I assume he thought was a non-intimidating and appealing way. They were like tongues or maybe tentacles. He lengthened them, twisted them, curled them around like a monkey's tail. This dude was an alien. That was freaking alien. And yet, my libido hadn't shut down. My inner core was still richly warm; the afterglow lapped at me like waves, slowing down the adrenaline that had risen with unveiling. After the initial surprise, I found myself still comfortable and safe with him—and curious.

I wanted to touch him. I wanted to please him like he had pleased me. I moved toward the edge of the bench, the water soaking my body, and he took a step closer toward me. He put his hand in my wet hair and directed my face toward his. I felt like a sexy vixen in that position, sitting between his widespread stance, staring up at him. It settled my resolve.

I dropped my gaze and stared down my opposition, this massive three-headed snake. It was still stubbornly erect. I put my hand underneath the rim of the head, pulling down over the other heads and shafts to his base in one long, slow motion. I felt his body shutter. The muscles in his thighs rippled. I pulled up, this time over the head. I didn't linger; quickly sliding my hand back down. He groaned. My hand didn't wrap entirely around his shaft, so I moved my wrist around freely to cover as much real estate as possible. Emboldened with the pulsing mass in my hand, I put his head into my mouth and rolled my tongue around it—its top, where it attached to the shaft, along the curve of it.

Drex braced himself against the shower walls and leaned over me, creating a shadow as he watched me suck on him. A growl escaped the back of his throat. His evident enjoyment encouraged me, and I braved a second hand on him. I twisted in the opposite direction of the first, creating friction as I pumped with my hands from his base to my mouth.

His cocks convulsed. His large hand grabbed my skull, presumably to encourage me to accept his seed. I wasn't sure about that. I wasn't even sure where it would come out. There was no way I'd be able to get all of his heads into my mouth, I didn't think. I kept working on the main one and rubbed my hands along the other two as Drex began to fight a bucking in his hips. He whispered my name, "Katy, Katy" in a warning as if I couldn't tell from his body that he was about to explode.

I shoved his head and part of his shaft into my mouth as it twitched violently. He nearly roared my name. He was obviously orgasming, reaching his peak, but I hadn't tasted anything. And my hands weren't any wetter as his bucking lessened. His body relaxed. I didn't let go even though it seemed to be over.

"Anything else?" I asked in a way that hopefully sounded more flirtatious than confused.

"Were you waiting for something?" he ribbed, grinning over the flowing water.

"No, I mean…sort of," I fumbled.

He pulled me up to him—his cock still erect—and gave me a massive kiss on the lips. "Human men ejaculate every time they orgasm, right? We don't. We have control. I figured you were already a bit worried about our anatomy. I didn't want to subject you to that. There is…a lot." Even saying it, he had a sly smile on his face.

"But you orgasmed?"

"I did," he said, his breathlessness confirming it. "The benefit of not ejaculating is that I can keep going for your pleasure. Shorter recovery period."

"What are the chances for pregnancy if you don't ejaculate?" I was suddenly curious about our options.

"Zero," he said simply.

"So, you're ready for me, like now?" I asked. The thought was fascinating.

"I am." His voice was silky.

Drex pumping nothing into my mouth was hotter than I expected, even though it had surprised me. I remained nervous about his size, but I didn't want our encounter to end yet. It would've been all I could think about until I experienced it. Curiosity killed the cat, or the pussy, I guessed. I led him to the pool.

Maybe we could cool off before attempting what I imagined was going to be a monumental feat. I used the seat as a step down and dunked myself. When I surfaced, I moved forward a bit so that my hair on the head was behind me and out of the way. When I opened my eyes, I got a big view of Drex. He had sat down on the edge of the dunk pool, with his feet on the inside seat. He had his legs spread and his penises were basically in my face. They had separated into their distinct entities, all connected at his body, close together. I got the image of tentacles searching for a place to sneak in and hide.

I moved forward toward his open legs, wide-eyed, trying to look at his face, although I will say the giant penises were distracting. He was gazing down at me, but I realized he was distracted too, the top half of my breasts were exposed and were vying for his attention. I rose a bit more so that he could see my nipples, and I gave them a little pinch to let him know that I was still pretty turned on. His penises lurched. I got close and ran my hands along his legs toward his crotch, then gave each head a wet kiss. I took his hands in mine and led him down into the water to sit on the bench. His penises reached around my belly before I backed away.

I wanted him to watch. First, I stood up on my tip toes so my breasts were mostly visible. I caressed them, letting them fall into the water, pulling them back up. Drex's deep dark eyes grew wide, and I heard a guttural purr from the back of his throat. Those tongues could make as many noises of pleasure as they made in mine.

I reached a hand down my front to touch myself, the water's surface distorting the view that Drex had. He watched intently as I explored my still lubricated folds in the warmth of the water. My fingers were so small compared to his, to his tongues, and to his dicks, but still it was appetizing as I did so under his powerful gaze. I relished in it, touching myself in front of a man that would only have what I wanted him to have.

Damn, I wanted him to take all of me.

I waded toward him, between his legs, and brought my face close to his. He pressed into me with a commanding, violent kiss with all of his tongues. His cocks had become rock hard. They moved erratically in the water, slapping my body, splashing us. I had him so turned on, and yet, he still made no motion to enter me. He put his hands on my arms to steady me against his forceful kissing, but he didn't hold me impossibly tight. I had an escape if I needed or wanted.

I didn't want to escape.

I moved closer. I put my hands on the back of his neck and dragged my breasts against his hard chest, as I climbed on top of his lap. I straddled his massive heat as they obediently pulled together. I desperately needed my breasts touched. I slid close to the base of his penises and pulled my mouth off of him, presenting my breasts instead. He took in a breast with his tongues, pressing swirls on my soft, wet skin. When his tongues pinched my nipple, my thighs clenched and I nearly orgasmed. And then before I could recover, he was onto the next breast, leaving the first sensitive and pink. I was desperate for him.

He gave my other breast just as much focused attention. My back arched, and I let out a small cry as he sucked with intensity. I refused to climax though. I pulled my breast from his mouth and gave him another kiss. I hoped he enjoyed my simple tongue. I was being blown away by his multiples. His thrusting penises I had pinned between my legs revealed I was doing just fine.

"I want you so bad, Katy," he muttered in between the smash of our mouths. He had gotten me so slick, even in the water, his hands on my hips, fingers clasping my ass cheeks.

I raised myself over him. "Just one at first," I requested in a whimper that was more desperate need than fear.

The dicks pulled apart, and he guided one toward my entrance. It played with my folds, slicked itself, turning me on even more. The thick head played outside my entrance, as if it was waiting for a formal invitation. I lowered myself on him and felt my entrance widen for his head and then tighten against his thick shaft. He filled me up and my eyes widened as I took more and more of him. He knocked his own head back, and I felt him lurch inside me, jolting me in the water. Had he orgasmed again? The thought of making this sexy man orgasm with a single slide into body empowered me. I bit my lip and lowered myself completely down, feeling absolutely speared. It twitched inside me, making my belly do somersaults. He maintained control of its movement inside me. It pivoted, probing for my spot. I cried out when he found it. Then he pounded on it until my eyes were clenched shut and my entire body was convulsing around his giant throbbing cock.

The penis underneath the one that was inside me had nestled in my butt crack and was thrusting in between my butt cheeks, wet and slick and stimulating my asshole without any penetration. I wondered if he had spilled lubrication or seed from it. Another dick pulsed steadily on my clit. I stroked it with my hand, running my fingers along it, pressing it between my hand and body so that it could feel like it was inside me too. Drex's arms were on my waist, keeping me grounded to his hips as he thrust inside me, rather than with his hips. He alternated between his eyes shut tight and intently staring at my face to get feedback on every new movement.

Soon I felt my hips thrusting despite myself. Old habits die hard, I guess as I added my own movement. I braced myself with his shoulders and held on as tight as I could. His muscles were so stiff, I couldn't dig my fingers into them. He gritted his teeth as I moved on top of him. He was getting close. I hoped so because I was desperately close to either reaching my peak or passing out with the need. There was so much pressure on my G-spot. His pulses quickened as he began to orgasm. My core clenched. A waterfall of electricity lit up my entire body. I choked out Drex's name as my channel clamped down on his cock. His lower rod pushed against my asshole, setting me alight, and every touch of my clit made my channel pulse hard against his cock until we both reached the peak of orgasms together, yelling out.

Our bodies fell limp with the exception of aftershocks which made the receiving person shudder.

I felt closer than ever to him as I collapsed onto his body in a toneless mass. His dick finally grew softer inside me. He gave me soft kisses on my face. They were perhaps to show gratitude, but it seemed like a natural extension of the passion and release we'd just experienced. He gave me soft kisses on my ear, his face lost in my hair that was wet-cold from being out of the water for so long.

After we had both caught our breath, I got off of him. With some small distance between our bodies, I was able to look into his face, and I was surprised how much joy it brought me. He looked more than just happy; he looked supremely content. And that's exactly how I felt. I mean, part of me was blown away by the best sex I'd ever had, but even after I felt really comfortable with him. Who knew I'd become *this* comfortable here, but Drex wasn't like any man I'd ever known. He would be way out of my league on Earth, but here, he was all mine, my host, and my insanely sexy adventure.

I used a washcloth to clean up the slickness on me before dunking my head to get my hair at least a good temperature as it was drying. Then, Drex showed me the heater which blew our skin and hair dry. A wonder I'd missed. His hands were still on me, keeping me close. He hung his clothes in the dryer and walked out in the buff. I'd forgotten I'd soaked his clothes. His ass was just as firm and tight as the rest of him, and I couldn't help but stare. His cocks could be seen hanging from behind too.

Sorry, not sorry.

I was in for a lot of trouble in these next months. And I was ready to accept my punishment.

He went into his room. I wasn't sure if we were going to just do separate things, so I wandered the living room for a moment. My question was answered as he rushed back into the room with a pair of lounge pants on. He scooped me up in his arms. I laughed, but his closeness was wonderful, especially after sex. All the feel-good hormones still floated around, and I wanted to be close to him, too. He sat us down on the couch, where we spooned and cuddled. And that was the second night that I fell asleep in his arms.

Chapter Sixteen
Plunge

Drex

I could hardly breathe as Katy led me into the pool room. I followed her luscious ass. It drove me crazy how I could only see hints of her figure in the loose clothing she had picked out. I craved seeing her lines, her waist dropping into that ass. I wanted to see her thick thighs again, those thighs that had squeezed my horns and my brain when I made her orgasm. Dang, I was already hard.

I almost lost it when she stripped for me. Her breasts were amazing, dew-dropped, and perfect. Her pink nipples popped on her light skin, and I wanted to squeeze them in my hands, feel their goodness. I wanted to touch all of her.

I didn't even realize I hadn't taken off any clothes when I walked into the shower with her. All I could see was her, her body, her amazingness. Her sly smile that she knew she had me in her grasps. I just wanted her in my arms. She drew close to me and took off my wet shirt, and I finally felt those breasts against my chest. Looking down at her, her body pressed against mine in the running of the shower was intense. My eyes ate up all of it, and my mind went a million places of how it wanted to see this image for the rest of my life. I saw us in hundreds of showers. I saw her back arching as she orgasmed in *our* bed. I saw us cuddling on the couch with whatever weird Earth show playing in the background. And in all of it, we had our eyes locked just like we did now.

As much as all those futures crashed into me, I forced myself to come back to the present moment. There was no promise she was going to be here in a few months. In fact, she had quite confidently said otherwise. I could only enjoy the moments I had now. And this moment was pretty dang good. I locked lips with her and let my worries melt away as my tongues wandered, and I got lost in her soft mouth. An occasional thrust of my tongue against hers hinted at what was next. I wanted to explore her wetness down there. My inhibited penises thrusted against my pants, trying to escape and find that deep wetness too.

I couldn't handle it anymore, and I could tell that she was getting uncomfortably hot, too. I scooped her up and gently put her on the slate bench. I dragged her sexy body to the edge of the seat and began devouring her pussy. It was impossibly sweet, and I was turned on by the patch of dark hair that hid her goodness from me. I dragged my tongue along her crevice, and she responded by grabbing my head. It was just what I wanted. I explored all of her with my tongues until she wept and panted. She quaked in my mouth with her orgasm and the most wonderful tastes and scents flooded me; I knew I'd be craving and imagining that sweet ambrosia for years to come. It was a new level of high. I felt the kick in my heart that made me shudder.

That rotha response to her scent, to her release, like my body was imprinting on her passion, driving me to please her over and over, as long as I lived.

If I thought she'd be satisfied and our playtime was over, I was quickly proven wrong as she began working the buttons on my pants. I pressed against the pants even more, making it tight without a lot of slack to work the buttons. She was not deterred though, and she managed the buttons with a small frantic panic that made me smile. I knew that human men only had one penis, and that they had very little control over it. However, I didn't anticipate how intense her reaction would be when they sprung from my clothing.

I couldn't tell if she was disgusted, disappointed, or upset. Maybe she was scared? I stepped back to give her space. I didn't want her to feel cornered.

After a few moments of confusion, she seemed to warm up to them. She touched them, and oh my, her soft hands and mouth were almost too much for me. Her mouth rolled over my head as her hands deftly rotated about the shafts. I wanted to pump my seed into her mouth, let it slide down her throat, as she drank me dry—but I also wanted to be ready for anything else she might have in mind. Plus, if she still harbored fear, then possibly squirting from all of them in terrible jets would not be best timed.

Before I could know it, she had me at the edge of my climax. I groaned deeply. As I came, I felt intense shudders in my chest. They were painful and harsh, but relieved with each pump of my penis into Katy's mouth as I orgasmed. And just as intense was Katy looking up at me from my dicks with those big eyes and wonderful smile. My human guest was pleased with herself for pleasing me. Once again, duty and obligation could not have led me to Katy's comfort, soft touch, and delicateness. This was something entirely separate.

Apparently, human abilities were quite different from ours, but I could tell that she was more curious than grossed out, so I was happy to answer her questions. She seemed especially excited that I was ready for more sex. While my sex life had been limited, from what I gathered and what I experienced, I couldn't imagine sex without multiple orgasms for all parties involved. I was ready for more of her, but as always, I remained respectful of Katy and her desires, even though I desperately wanted to tear into her with my cocks until she was screaming, yanking my horns, and receiving jets of hot cum in all her holes.

But Katy also seemed to want more. She dunked down into the water. I loved watching her surface. I admired her breasts in the water, and her long hair floating like a long veil behind her. She was absolutely gorgeous. And my heart gave a dull ache, thankfully not a painful sting. I was sure now that they were rotha pangs, but I also had no idea what to do with that information.

I joined her in the pool at her request. I put my hands on her hips and I never wanted to let go. More kisses, more wonderfulness. This woman was absolutely amazing. She climbed on top of me, and I finally got to put my mouth on those breasts again. I sucked on her nipples to make them into tight peaks on her perfect mounds. She whimpered and muttered soft noises in my ear as she played with my horns, and we enjoyed such intimacy.

Then it was more than I dared to ask. She moved to have me enter her. A single cock would be enough for her at first. I knew from my tongue and my fingers that her space was tight and small. I felt her entrance give for the head of my cock and then absolutely swallow it, tightening down my shaft. We went intensely slow, inching in. I felt the sides of her cavern ripple with pleasure as I explored, pivoting my head inside her, giving her pleasure in every direction. I found a particular spot behind her clit and used that to my advantage, watching her body jolt with every touch of that sensitive area. Meanwhile, my other cocks were in ecstasy too, the lower rubbing between her butt cheeks, the higher dancing around what she told me was her clit, a wonderful button accessible from the outside to give what I hoped was a crown of pleasure to her entire area.

Soon she was crudely bouncing on my dick. I loved the shifting weight of her body in the pool. She made waves as my own pleasure began to undulate. I began to lose focus, the world spinning. I was lost in Katy. I was lost in the abyss. Her cries stirred a frenzy. I orgasmed, too. I shuddered inside her. Her body and climax crashed into mine as we became one. Deep inside her, I felt a part of her. She was amazing. I held her in the water and wished a million times that we'd never separate. There, for a moment, with her, I didn't feel any burdens. There, I had just a moment to be with her. And that honestly made me feel like the luckiest man in the galaxy. These stolen moments were better than anything else I would ever experience in my life. I wanted her. All of her. Forever.

Chapter Seventeen
Photos

Katy

While I was settling in nicely with Drex in Xavia, there were still plenty of reminders of Earth. Drex had Davian transfer my video files to the Xavian settit. Much to my embarrassment, he made them available as a library for everyone, but I heard from the other women that they were thankful to have something from home to watch. They showed their hosts of life on Earth, even if it was in the form of sitcoms and dramedies.

It was strange, but the humans began to look at me as sort of a leader. I guess because I happened to be hosted by Drex, the prince. I talked to them all and got to know them through the settit. I suggested they send in any media they had so we could get a larger library of videos that wasn't just my collection. I also spent more time with individual Xavians because of my job. I took photos of Gulshan working tapestry, and of Lowree making jewelry. When I showed Drex the photographs I had taken, he suggested I show them to everyone.

"We can't gather, but the settit allows everyone to be connected at once for announcements. It could be like a gallery or show."

"Oh, I don't know about that…" I said, nervous by the mere suggestion of it. Speaking to the women individually to make sure they were comfortable or snapping some photos one-on-one with a friendly Xavian was one thing. Showcasing my work was an entirely different thing.

"They are wonderful, and I think it will bring us some joy."

I'm sure Drex was happy for me and wanted to show my work off, but it was his job to think optimistically. These photographs were of an endangered culture—even he had said that—and the Xavians could find it incredibly disrespectful or dense.

"What if they don't like them?" I asked. I tried to communicate my nervousness to him. Wedding photography had its stress too. There was always the fear you'd missed an important photo. Mostly, it was about having a million photos to capture everything.

"Of course, they will like them, and they will appreciate them." Drex thought they were wonderful, but he had also gotten to put his penis inside me, so I assumed his opinion was slightly biased.

I tried my best to explain it to Drex, fumbling through most of my reasons.

"I thought this was your job on Earth," he said.

I'm sure he was a bit confused because I had asked for a job and now, I was suddenly nervous about showing anyone the fruits of my labor. Still, with the culture and language barriers, this could go terribly.

"My job on Earth never had such a broad and important audience," I said.

"You're analyzing this too much. Xavians have so little. We appreciate what we do have. They will appreciate this."

I looked over the photos. I captured Lowree's delicate hands. I captured a great shot of Gulshan teaching several bulky men how to weave on a loom. It was sad that there had been so much tragedy here, but there was also still good. It was impossible for my photography to *not* capture that, at least in some way. I took photos of what was there, pure evidence. Sometimes, it told more truth than one could see in the moment, but it never lied. One had to acknowledge photographic evidence. I wanted to tell the Xavians that they had happened. That I saw them.

I agreed.

Chapter Eighteen
Business

Drex

I sat behind my desk, elbows on the arm rests, my fingers tented in front of me, as I discussed with Davian and Vance official matters. It was actually rather boring, which was how I preferred it. The Orkain had been quiet recently. We were still trying to learn more about them. One of our military leaders, Chelk, had taken a small contingent north toward the caves in an attempt to locate the Orkain's home base. They had found signs of activity, which would dictate how the next expedition would be led.

We also discussed any issues regarding our human guests. They all expressed relative contentment in their locations, but we knew that was not enough. Being comfortable in a home was very different from establishing a romantic pairing. If we had a safe place to gather, we could have more natural meetings and interactions between the males and the females. Unfortunately, that wasn't the case, and things had to be more deliberate. No one had asked to live with a different, particular host, but that's what we needed.

After safety, we needed chemistry. We needed what Sara and Vance had, what Katy and I had.

After the matters of the state had been discussed, Davian exited the conversation, and Vance and I had a moment to catch up privately.

"So, things are going well between you and Katy, I take it?" Vance had a giant grin on his face. It probably matched my own. I wasn't one to kiss and tell, but it was sort of a government matter, wasn't it?

"Yes, you could say that. It took some time to understand her wants—"

"That bad at it, are you?" Vance ribbed.

"No! I mean she wanted that job. She cares for her sister. She has struggles, but I am really enjoying her company and getting to know her." And I was honest about that. Katy was nothing like I had imagined. Experiencing rotha with a random human…I would not be able to explain it. I was in over my head, but there was no way I was going to pass up an opportunity to enjoy Katy and bring her some comfort in this messed up situation she was in. I wanted whatever she wanted.

"I'm glad things are working out for you. Sara and I might have an announcement soon." He waggled his eyebrows which made the nubs around his hairline move.

"What sort of announcement?" I asked. Could it be that he was experiencing rotha as well? Or, could Sara be pregnant?

"You'll just have to wait and find out. I shouldn't have even said that much," he laughed.

Chapter Nineteen
Tease

Katy

I had been in Drex's room several times now, although besides our naps, I had us still roughly sleeping in separate rooms. I wanted Drex to know that this was a lot of fun, but it wasn't staying. His room was decorated much like the rest of the house, minimal, slate-colored, but cozy. My room was the only room that was a rough copy of something from Earth in a sweet attempt to make me comfortable.

The first time I was in his room, Drex carried me over the threshold after a huge make-out session on the couch. I think he wanted a proper place to bed me. He had a long bed with a nightstand on either side of the bed, which made me think that he was hoping someone would be sleeping with him when he built his house. I wondered vaguely if he had ever had someone in mind. I wondered if he ever considered he'd be with an alien woman. My thoughts on what ifs faded as Drex placed me gently on the bed and then climbed on top of me, expressing in kisses what he wanted to do all of me. Our mouths only separated to take off my blouse. His large hands surrounded my breasts, squeezing softly. His mouth moved to my neck and nibbled my collarbone.

I loved the way he played with my body, covering it with open wet kisses, lapping at my skin with his tongues. I yanked off his shirt and moved my hands over his body too, but he only tolerated so much of it. He was busy pleasuring me, busy making me feel amazing, busy making me shiver with anticipation. He deftly unbuttoned my pants with his freaking tongues. He stared me down while doing so, as if stating, "If I can undo these buttons, just think how I'm going to undo you."

I grabbed handfuls of his hair and ran my fingers through it. He gave a little hum of pleasure as he pulled off my pants to find my panties growing a large wet spot, and getting wetter by the moment as he breathed hot air between my legs. He gave my panties a wide lick before roughly pulling them down to my knees, twisting them and binding my legs close together despite me wanting to open wide to him. A heavy arm on either side held my legs close together, leaving my clit available and on full display.

Drex

With each gentle pulse of my tongue, I unhooded that button of pleasure, that precious pearl. I could suck on it all day, listen to her cum all day. I felt her legs twitch underneath me. She wanted more. She thrust against my tongue, but I wasn't ready for her to cum just yet. I lessened the pressure, re-hooded that button, and grabbed handfuls of ass. I controlled her body. I controlled her pleasure.

With a flick of my tongue, I lifted off her clit and let a long hot breath escape over it. She giggled in relief, but then gasped as one of my tongues slipped down below her clit, in between her closed legs, grazing her legs and her folds as another tongue made wide rainbows above her clit. Katy trembled, but she didn't cum.

Katy

The bed was becoming damp; I was unbelievably wet. The tongues swiping between my closed legs was such a turn-on. He had me pinned, teasing my lower half into a tangle of maddening desire. Could he not see that I was more than ready? My legs struggled underneath him, and every time I thought I might get a quick release, he would back off, leaving me panting and needing him even more. I wanted his cock. I wanted him inside me. I thought he might torture me with foreplay forever. I was dripping for him, and my moans were quickly becoming frustrated noises. I never wanted anything more in my life. I wanted to feel that thick cock inside me. Why wouldn't he give it to me?

Even though he wasn't looking at me, I could tell by the pull of his lips—he was amused by the control he had over my pleasure…or suffering, as it were. I gave him a playful smack on his shoulder, the only part besides his head I could reach. Upon my turn to violence, he looked up and couldn't even keep a straight face. He gave a huge grin. He knew what he was doing. He bound up my legs in his arms and dragged the underside of his tongue over my clit, between my legs, and then a sly coil against my asshole. Dude could basically swallow me. And I wanted it bad.

I think he knew he had reached his limit or my limit, as it was. He pulled my panties off. Now free, I opened my legs and presented my sopping wet pussy.

My fingers arrived to explore my wetness. I was tender, swollen, and soaked. I played with myself as I watched Drex undo his pants, anxious to see those cocks spring out from the clothing that bound them. I was always amazed so much fit into those pants. When they were finally set free, they were long, hard, and green with a twist that pulled them together.

He watched my fingers play with my pussy, sliding through the folds, two fingers twirling over my clit. On his way over my body, his mouth found my breasts—sucked the nipples into tight peaks—before his green horned face was on mine. His cock dragged against my leg before separating into three exploring and rubbing against my wetness.

It felt like more teasing to me. I needed one of those cocks inside me now. Right now. I put my hand down there and grabbed the biggest one and began to guide it inside.

"You need me?" he asked, pausing to take in my desperate answer and plea.

"Yes, please. I need you."

He watched my face as he pushed slowly into my body. It was what I desperately needed, and yet my channel was so tight. He was attentive; he rested for a moment to let my body adjust and accept the massive cock. With a couple of long, gentle thrusts, he was able to stretch me, and I felt waves of pleasure through my core. I felt his grunts of pleasure as he stretched my limits.

The smaller rod stiffened along my clit. With each thrust, his lower dick pressed onto my closed asshole, applying a pressure that felt a bit strange, but quickly became enticing. I loved the tease, and with each pulse, he opened my asshole bit by bit until I suddenly found myself needing that dick, too.

He asked consent with his eyes, and I nodded, a little lost in the pleasure and ready to explore. He pressed gently but steadily through the resistance, until I felt the relief of his head having entered. It stung, but it also sent pleasure in tingles and waves. It was easier once he got the head in, and the feel of the shaft moving along the rim of my asshole made my body convulse in bliss. As he got deeper, I thought it would hurt more, but it didn't. What I wasn't expecting was the steady pleasant pressure on my pussy. Soon I was so full. Spots lit up where I never knew they existed. I clawed at his shoulders. It was so hot, and it was so good.

I could tell he was getting close too. His movements were becoming less controlled. He gritted his teeth, set his jaw, desperate to hold on until I was at my very edge. I couldn't imagine going much longer. The feelings were so new and intense and had built up so fast, faster than I intended. The anticipation had killed some of the time, but it was worth it. I felt such a desperate need to orgasm. I gasped for air, my heart threatened to pound out of my chest, and there was so much pressure on my G-spot.

I cursed loudly. I told him he was going to make me cum. I wanted him to cum with me. "Will you cum in my ass?" I asked.

"Yeah?" he said. I knew he had heard me, he just wanted to hear more. He was already breathless, trying to hold back.

"I need you to cum in my ass!" I cried.

Fuck, that was all he needed.

His arms tightened around my sides, as his pelvis involuntarily thrust. His lower dick throbbed and shuddered hot, powerful streams into my ass, while he dry-pumped into my vagina, making me feel like I was being filled to the brim in both, and it was double the pleasure as I came alongside him. My walls squeezed him tight until I had wrung all the pleasure from my core, until I was utterly and completely spent, and we were just softly thrusting into oblivion. His horned head leaned against mine. We were both damp with the exertion, and when he pulled out of me and my holes retracted and closed, I felt heavy with pleasure. I felt heavy with his cum. He collapsed beside me and nuzzled my face with his—as we both lay there, boneless, and utterly spent.

Chapter Twenty
Two Bedrooms

Drex

My first instinct was to pull her tighter to me when she stirred in my bed. I wrapped my strong legs around her cool ones. It was always comforting to warm her body at any time of the day or night, another form of love and affection. I loved the way my arms wrapped around the curve of her hips. I loved the way her head fit on my chest. I enjoyed how well we fit together. She responded with a quick snuggle back, her arms gave me a squeeze. I was just about to doze off again, as she began disentangling herself from my limbs and sheets.

"Just sleep here," I coaxed. The sex had been so wonderful, and we had fallen asleep in each other's arms. I just wanted it to continue. I wished she would stay—even if it wouldn't be forever. Morning couldn't be that far away.

Against my reluctant body, she finally extricated herself. I didn't have to open my eyes to know she remained close. Her hair fell upon my face as she landed a thick, heavy kiss on my mouth. Instantly, my soul sprang to life. She moved me in so many ways. I did not open my eyes because I did not want to watch her leave.

As expected, her weight disappeared from the bed even as her scent lingered. The spot where she'd slept would grow cool. I heard her gentle padding of feet, and the click of the door which signaled another middle-of-the-night escape of my love. I stretched on the now too-big bed, but I'd much rather be squished against her.

The rotha felt the emptiness too and struck out to notify me Katy had left, as if I didn't know. In the last weeks, my need for her had grown. That struggle in my chest had become a punishment when I wasn't around her. She had been the only thing to bring me comfort, and only when she was close. I'd heard of rotha mates who did not join together. It'd been of biological detriment to the individuals, but sometimes it had been chosen, all the same. I knew this pain wouldn't be going away soon, as I knew it had not left Katy.

Katy's Earth rotha may have left, but that didn't mean he wouldn't return, and when he did, she'd have trouble being with anyone else. She would go to him, and she would be happy. I was a placeholder. I might have been okay with that; I was okay with that. I had only agreed to this hosting because of the image I had to keep for the good of my people. I enjoyed her carefree company, her dedication to work, but now my own fate had made itself known. I hadn't known mismatched fates could happen, but she was from another world. Maybe things didn't work seamlessly when it came to a galaxy of interspecies rotha. I was fated to her. And I could tell by the pain she felt, that she was fated to him. Otherwise, why not stay?

Sleep wasn't making its return. My heart felt heavy, and not just because of the rotha. I truly missed her. I knew she had the right to leave in the middle of the night. She'd be leaving for the other side of the galaxy, too. She did not plan to become a mother of alien children. Complex reasons had brought us together and would soon pull us apart, but my body and my zarata cared not.

And that was why I'd already lost. That was why I already mourned. Because as long as Katy was rotha to someone else, she would feel the same way. Her mate would return. The stars would see to it. The fates. Her marriage was inevitable. My loss and grief were also inevitable. Perhaps she already understood it. I had to understand it.

I didn't want to understand it. I wanted nothing more than to care for her for the rest of my life. I'd hold her tight, protect her, and love her, despite her destiny elsewhere.

And yet, I slept alone.

Chapter Twenty-One
Mixed Signals

Katy

I woke up angry with myself, alone in the bed that was always cold. I both hated that I had left Drex's bed, and that I had fallen asleep there in the first place. At least I had the sense to return to my room. As much as I enjoyed his company in bed, I wasn't going to stay and be his lifetime mate. I was leaving. So, I tried to keep a little distance, even if I couldn't stop myself from passionately throwing myself upon him every chance.

I'd never been very sexual, but Drex had awakened something in me. I mean, obviously, the dude had three dicks, but there was something electric about his touch that drove me wild. I felt the intensity of his want, of his desire to treat me well, like I was the only one he would ever care about or want. It was the ferocity with which he goes after me. And, I mean, we can chalk that up to not having enough females on his planet, but still, it felt like something more, a lingering touch, the look in his eye. It was not just about physical sensations. There was a connection that we teased, and as much as I should stay away, I truly cannot get enough. And so, needless to say, the sex had been wonderful.

That connection scared me too. I didn't want him to interpret it and the sex, and think I was going to fall madly in love with him. I wasn't here to do that. He verbalized understanding it, but my government had promised him otherwise, and I was sexing him up. I could see how signals could get crossed.

I had too much going on. I had to get back to Earth. I had to pick up the pieces of my life. Perhaps it was too much to ask Drex to understand about being abandoned at the altar. Perhaps, it was unfair. Didn't he think he was getting a lifetime mate waltzing off of the ship and into his arms? I wasn't that. I was never going to be that. I didn't know if he understood that. He had been nothing but respectful of me and the rest of the women, so I struggled to reconcile his expectations and his treatment of us. At the very least, I needed to maintain *some* distance, even if it was sleeping the rest of the night in my bedroom after an admittedly outstanding romp and rollick.

Chapter Twenty-Two
Showcase

Drex

Katy looked gorgeous in an elegant dress of heavy fabric which dripped over the curves of her body. The low V neckline showcased her sumptuous cleavage and the necklace I gave her for the occasion, a big single pearl held to a thin chain with gold. Handcrafted by one of the jewelers, it was a fine piece, but it looked even finer against her fair skin. Her smile wavered with nervousness as we approached time for her presentation. I hadn't a moment to reassure her as her sister unattached herself from Vance and had pounced on her. They spoke so quickly; I was unable to translate any of it.

Instead, Vance and I went into the kitchen to pour fage for ourselves and the ladies.

"How are things going?" he asked. Since we worked together every day, I knew this question was really, 'How are things going between you and Katy?'

I gave a weak smile. I was always honest with my best counsel, but it was difficult in this regard, given how well things were going for him and Sara. They'd been thoroughly enjoying each other's company, and it was a little awkward knowing that he'd probably share with Sara anything I told him in these moments.

"It seems things are going well. You always know how to put up a good image though, have you impregnated her yet?" he asked bluntly.

"No, but we've had sex," I offered quickly, caught off guard.

"You got to get on that," he said. "If she's anything like her sister…"

I didn't know where he was going with that, and I didn't want to know. Sex with Katy was amazing, but I wasn't sure if she was going to stay when given the chance to leave. I wasn't about to ask her about having a baby and ruining whatever chance I had to keep her. More than a vessel for a baby, she was my rotha.

Ready to be done with the conversation, I walked the drinks into the living room. Sara was quick to grab hers, then she grabbed her man, entwining their arms. She was adorably small next to Vance, who always boasted his shoulders and chest were bigger than even mine.

"A toast?" I asked as I handed Katy her glass. Katy stood close to me, and I put my hand on her back. We at least looked like a couple, too.

Vance and Sara looked at each other and shared smiles. "Should we?" she asked.

Vance nodded and his smile broke into a grin. "Yes, a toast to rotha," he said.

I was taken aback. How did he know about my fating?

Vance and Sara separated their arms to reveal their palms. On their palms were matching markings, just a shade redder than their respective skin. It was faint currently, but it was obviously a rotha mark.

"What is that?" asked Katy, she handed me her drink as she took Sara's palm in both of her hands. She tried to rub it off.

"You haven't told her?" Vance asked dumbly.

"I have," I said. Even I recognized the agitation in my voice. Was it anger? Jealousy? I directed my words to Katy, "Remember I told you about my parents and how rotha manifested as marks up the arms? This is the start of that."

Katy gasped. She looked at Sara. She looked at Vance. She looked at me, trying to process it all.

"I'm sure your markings will show up soon," said Sara, trying to be helpful.

Katy actually looked at her palms to see if there indeed was something forming on them. There was nothing. I knew there was nothing. She hadn't had any hints of rotha, and I had hoped it was a species-thing, but it was just that, she wasn't rotha to me. She was fated to another.

Vance gave a little cough. And it brought me back to the situation at hand. I could be political. I could be proper.

"Congratulations Vance. Congratulations Sara." I handed Katy her glass back and we all toasted, although Katy still seemed a little lost.

"We are going to have the ceremony," said Vance.

"It's sort of like an engagement party," explained Sara to Katy. "It's an announcement to the village that we've found each other and are living our lives together."

Katy gave a weak smile, and I knew she was thinking about her own failed ceremony.

"I'm happy for you," she said timidly, and then gave her sister a hug. The hug was returned tightly until I could see Katy warm to it. "I really am happy for you," she repeated.

Both women had tears in their eyes. Humans appeared to be just as confusing and complicated as my own people. Katy wanted to be happy for her sister, but it was a lot of information to take in, and probably also made her sad. I hated that for her. She was about to present to the entire village through the communicators, and her sister had just announced massive personal news.

I thought about it. If Sara was rotha, she would be staying. What did that mean for Katy? Would she stay with her sister, or would she return to her Earth?

Katy took a big gulp of fage and busied herself re-arranging loom-weaving photographs, before returning them to their original locations. She was gathering herself. I gave her a moment. I spoke with Vance and Sara about the details of the ceremony. Sara wanted Katy to take photographs. Vance asked me to stand with them for support. The rest of the village would be on settit. Vance and Sara would be our first successful 'coupling' and hopefully babies would follow. It was good public relations.

"No baby yet," Sara answered my unasked question. "Otherwise, I wouldn't be downing this fage."

"What do you mean?" asked both Vance and myself.

"I assume this wouldn't be good for the baby, like alcohol."

I remembered Katy calling the fage alcohol.

"It won't hurt the baby," said Vance. "In fact, it's important for you to feel happy, most especially when pregnant."

"Oh, I like the sound of that," Sara said. She took another big sip.

"When do you want to do the ceremony?" I asked Vance.

"As soon as possible. We can't wait to share the good news."

I agreed with him. While I was trying to be respectful of everyone's privacy, I knew others were very interested in how the program was going. I didn't feel comfortable sharing my experiences because they weren't going well, so it would be good to share Vance's and Sara's.

Katy took another sip of fage as she gave me a look, like she was playfully exasperated with her sister already. I enjoyed being in on the joke. Her sister had wanted to share her good news, and she wanted to do it in person, but it was all a bit much, especially on a day and event that was supposed to be about Katy's work. I wondered how much this sort of dynamic played out. I wondered if Sara would have left Earth to be with her sister, like Katy had so easily done. Katy was a strong and thoughtful woman.

I was proud of her. Even if it was all going to collapse in a few months. I was honored to have her in my home. I wished more than anything I could keep her as mine. I would take care of her every need, and we would spend every waking moment in bed, in each other's arms, or however the sex position of the moment dictated.

When the program started, she was amazing. She expressed gratefulness to everyone for allowing her the opportunity to photograph them. Everyone was impressed by the photos as I had been. She had captured us well.

At the start and closing of the presentation, she brought me in and kept me close. I was thankful to not experience any rotha pain during those times. Selfishly, I didn't want others to know I was experiencing rotha, because when she left—they'd know something had gone terribly wrong. They'd know I wasn't fit to be a mate, and possibly not to be their leader.

While it remained respectfully unspoken, I know my people were appreciative of this record and legacy, especially with things at risk. I wished we had done this much earlier, before we had lost so many people, but at least we had it now. It was a wonderful gift Katy had given us. I would be forever grateful for her.

Katy

I thought the showcase went well. I was proud of my work. The Xavian people deserved my best, even if they were going to take my sister from me.

When I first saw the marks on Sara, I thought they were a trick. Maybe Vance was being deceptive, playing some sort of mind-game on Sara, and marking her in her sleep. I guessed the betrayal from my own government and former loves fueled that concern. I had to wonder how much else of this was planned or contrived. But Drex seemed just as surprised as I was that Sara was showing the marks of rotha. I trusted him, and decided this was a really, really weird thing, but it wasn't a trick.

I didn't think living on Xavia and interacting with its people could physically change our bodies. It was like her genes were expressing different things because she was in a different environment. Was it the fact that they had physical sex? I had sex with Drex, an alien, multiple times. I hadn't sensed any changes in my body. I had a bitter passing thought that of course, it would happen to Sara, and not to me. My life seemed to have a pattern of being passed over.

I didn't know how yet, but I knew this would change things for me, Sara, and any chance of a return trip to Earth. It was like the planet was claiming her. I tried my best to put the thoughts out of my mind, but even after Vance and Sara had left, I was too amped to go to bed. The rush from the nervousness and the surprise from my sister left too many thoughts rattling around in my head. I invited Drex to watch some episodes of *Telefunctional* with me. He was quiet. I didn't know if he was being respectful of me, or if he also didn't want to talk about the rotha pairing of my sister and his best friend. It was like one of those elephants in the corner, type-things. Drex and I had met at the same time that Vance and Sara had met. We were sort of on the same timeline and same circumstances. If it were a race, we were clearly behind. I didn't even know if we were on the track, at this point. Maybe we were just in the stands.

Still, I found a lot of comfort, lying on his chest with his arms wrapped around me. I felt safe, even if maybe it wasn't fair to him. Maybe he wished he wasn't on the stands. Maybe he wished he was comparing rotha markings with me. I was too scared to ask. Mostly, because I wouldn't know what to do with that information. How could we continue what we were doing when I learned the truth—whatever that truth was? So, I stayed quiet. And he stayed quiet. Maybe we were at the cusp of an end.

We watched several episodes of *Telefunctional* before I passed out, including one of my favorite ones when the main character had to call another call center as a customer. I woke up when Drex got up from underneath me. I stood up automatically to go to bed with him. He took my hand in my sleepy state and walked me down the hallway. There he gave me a kiss, reminding me that we would be separating from here.

I put my hands on his shoulders and stood on my tiptoes to give him another kiss. Even in my sleepy state, I felt him wince. Our goodnight kisses were different from all the other kisses. They seemed painful. He turned away and went into his room, leaving me there in the hallway. I know he was only doing it because of the precedents *I* had set, but still, it hurt. Perhaps it hurt him just as much when I left the bedroom in the middle of the night. In the end, love always brought a harmful sting. I went to bed, but I was wide awake, lost in my thoughts. Maybe I was reading too much into things. Maybe he did just enjoy the sex. Maybe he did just want a sex partner. Maybe he was content with the arrangement as it was. And what could I demand? Nothing. Because I was leaving.

Chapter Twenty-Three
Kumirata

Katy

A week later, workers bustled in and out Drex's house to prepare for the kumirata, or fating ceremony. The lighting, audio equipment, and decorations made for a cramped affair in Drex's small home. It was the first one since they'd scattered from their larger dwellings, so it was quickly becoming a village-affair. Having it in the prince's home showed his support.

Drex's people came in with the largest flowers I had ever seen. They were the size of elephant ears. I'd seen flowers like them on a smaller scale near the house, but they must have looked far for these gigantic ones. Someone else brought in a wedding arch of delicately woven vines and flowers—the shape wasn't something I'd seen in Xavian culture, so I knew it had been Sara's idea, but the way the flowers and vines were woven had taken the work of several people and wasn't anything like I'd seen before. It was delightful. Given it was the first cross-species kumirata, it had been up to Vance and Sara to figure out how they wanted to handle things. The only thing Sara had to draw on was

American weddings; I wished that hadn't been the case. I think I could have handled a foreign ceremony a lot better.

Honestly, I'd been annoyed when she'd allowed Vance to announce the news just prior to me going on stage in front of the entire village. I didn't say anything, though. I wondered how many people had felt hurt when I talked about my previous engagement. I had wanted everyone to share in my good news. I hadn't thought too much about how other people might struggle with the news based on their own history and relationships with people. I promised myself to be more considerate, rather than to confront my sister over hers. Besides, I had figured it just as inconsiderate to bring up my ex-fiancé during *her* good news. I didn't want to seem wrapped up in it, still. It felt especially dumb, given it had occurred on an entirely different planet.

Sara got ready in my bedroom. I helped her dress and did her makeup and her hair. Our roles were now reversed, but she was already ahead because her future person had arrived—accompanied her, even. He was here. Perhaps that's what I should have done. Screw not seeing the bride before the ceremony; he should have driven me there. Yeah, definitely not still wrapped up in it, I told myself.

I moved around her, braiding the front pieces of her hair with delicate flowered vines and tying them in the back so they appeared as a tiara. The dress she'd picked out was gorgeous, dyed purple from some plants in a method I had documented firsthand in my photographs. Sara had developed a good relationship with the seamster, Bolin, and he'd altered and adorned the dress with beading in just a few days for Sara.

"Isn't this wonderful?" asked Sara, her eyes glassy with tears.

Honestly, I didn't know how this would turn out. Sara was only a few years younger than me, but she had had several intense, whirlwind relationships. She'd never tried to marry any of them, thankfully. I'd been the only one to try to make that mistake. Besides being to an alien, this relationship did seem different. Who was I to argue with this fating stuff?

"You guys seem really happy," I said. The markings on her palm had gotten even darker in the last week. At a distance, they could pass as freckles, but upon closer inspection, they were tiny swirls—points of some alien design. Better for it to happen to her.

I put aside my issues and enjoyed spending time with Sara. If I'd stayed on Earth, I wouldn't have known if she was safe or even alive. And here I got to experience her happiness firsthand. I didn't regret a moment of it so far. While I thought Sara's brash ideas were inadvisable, I wasn't actually as worried as maybe I would have been on Earth. Drex's people had shown us nothing but kindness, even when they had been duped by our government. I mean, this hadn't been the craziest idea my sister ever had…just last year she had decided to fly off into space and meet the Xavian people. This just felt like the next weird step in her life. Also, if I decided to leave, I'd feel more comfortable knowing someone felt at least some amount of dedication to her. That was the whole point of me coming, to make sure that she was going to be safe and happy, not to prevent it. I'd miss her, though.

When I considered what I missed on Earth, it wasn't much. Sara was here, and she was most of what

I had enjoyed on Earth. She was my only family. She was my best friend. My work wouldn't be missed. My photos competed with billions of other photos. There were plenty of people to capture the culture of Earth. Here, my work was important.

I snapped another photo of her and looked at it on the device's monitor. I noticed a shadow around her belly. I checked the woman I'd just photographed. She caught me eyeing her.

"I might be," she said. It'd only been a week since we'd last seen each other, but I could tell she'd been on the lookout for signs herself. She gave a cheerful little shrug. "Today first, though."

She meant she wanted this day to be about her and Vance. I couldn't blame her for that. If she was pregnant, there wouldn't be much more alone time for them. And I imagined there would be even more babies to come, because that was the point, right? Make them happy. Get them pregnant. Continue the species.

Mike and I had wanted to have a family—another mind-boggling facet I'd spent too much time thinking about after. I imagined he'd have family without me. He was in a new relationship already, but I tried not to follow his life too closely. I had to grieve. I had to separate emotionally from him. Eventually, it had been time for me to set off on my own. Maybe the spaceship had been a bit much, though.

Still, kumirata and possible pregnancy? I was terrified for my sister. Excited, but terrified. How long would she be pregnant? Would the baby be viable? Sara was a brave woman, rushing head-long into this. I admired her leaps of faith, but I wasn't sure if I envied her position. It all seemed to work out for her, though.

I felt done with my leaps. Sure, I'd gotten on a spaceship to visit an alien planet, but I had done it for very exacting reasons. And, I was definitely going to second-think anything like this again. Flying leaps and trust might work well for Sara, but I needed to learn to trust in myself and make my own decisions.

I had put out light snacks. There was a giant jug of fage as well. I drank plenty of it to keep me on the festive side of the ceremony and my thoughts.

At the start of the ceremony, Sara and Vance walked on screen from opposite sides and me in the middle. Vance wore a burgundy leather vest over his broad chest and matching slacks. They held each other's hands and eye contact, as if no one else existed in the world. I hovered behind the cameras, helping with the broadcast to the hundreds of Xavians watching on their settits.

Drex stood behind them and spoke. "I've known Vance since we were both children. Vance has always been dutiful to not only serve his people, but to prepare for his rotha. And despite the tragedies that have befallen us, he found Sara across this galaxy of romance and possibility. Sara traveled the far reaches of space to find where she might belong, and she has found Vance. They belong together. The fates have called it; rotha hasn't abandoned us yet. We are here to support this couple as best we can. Please join us," said Drex.

Listening to Drex made me cry. I knew if I left that he would still be here to watch out for Sara and support her relationship. That touched me more than I expected.

Vance and Sara kissed as Drex stepped away. I wasn't sure if that was part of their ceremony or if it was ours, but it was a lovely touch. I had never seen Sara so happy. She was more than in love. This did seem more like fate.

Chapter Twenty-Four
Quietly

Katy

At the end of the evening, when all the fage had gone, Vance and Drex stepped outside to scout the skies. There hadn't been a violent incident since the day we had landed. I might have been getting complacent, but not on a day like today. I was a catastrophizer. And for Vance and Drex, it was a way of life.

With the focus on the kumirata and Sara, I had hoped to escape it, but the inevitable question was…unavoidable.

"How are you two doing?" Sara asked.

I gave a smile. It was too complicated to talk about at evening's end. "I'm definitely enjoying his company," I offered.

Sara's eyebrows rose as she read between the lines. "I'm glad you are getting some, sis!"

I blushed, even though she'd been basking in the alien afterglow since we'd arrived on Xavia.

"And I'm glad you're really happy," I said as I gave her a hug and held her close. "That's why I came here to make sure you'd be okay." I didn't want her to think that just because I was sleeping with Drex that I was staying. "That doesn't necessarily change my plans, you know. I'm supposed to go back to Earth."

"No!" she shouted, surprised, pulling part way out of the hug.

"I accompanied you to make sure you were safe and happy. You are. Maybe they'll let me visit."

"But what about Drex?"

See. I knew she expected me to change my plans because of a man. I wasn't doing that again. "What about him? He is a nice man. He gives me the best orgasms of my life," I said bluntly, my shyness giving way to indignation. "But I can't make life decisions based on being with a man for a few months. I have to make decisions for me, not for *love*, not for someone else. We saw how that turned out last time."

"Not all men are like that, Katy. He's not even *human*. He can't be any more different from your ex."

"Part of being 'over Mike' is about not repeating the same mistake. I can't throw away my life on Earth, because of someone—*anyone*—else. It has to be because of *me*."

"How do you know that jumping into this *isn't* for *you*? How do you know you're not denying what you want, just for the sake of what? Practicality?" she retorted.

I didn't have an answer for her. I'm glad she could jump into something, but maybe I needed to not-jump. I needed to make the best decisions for myself, even if she didn't understand them. Drex needed a partner, someone to keep up the royal gig and give him babies. How could I know that Drex liked me for who I was, and not just for what I could give him? I was done being on someone else's whim, for someone else's benefit.

Before I could voice my concern, the men returned. Vance made a bee line to his rotha and embraced her. I gave my sister a "be quiet" look, but she wasn't looking at me anymore.

"They're staying the night. We spotted two Orkain out there," said Drex.

"We can stay in your old bedroom!" said Sara under pretense the room wasn't being used by me.

Drex gave me a consolatory look as I left to give the room a cursory tidy for our guests. Sara and I had gotten ready in the room, so it was a bit cluttered. I cleared off the bed and made room on some of the horizontal surfaces for what I hoped were their belongings, and not for their bodies. Oh well, it was their first official night. Honeymoon? They could have some fun. I took out clothing for myself that night and for the morning, and then left the room for them.

After ensuring my guests were comfortable for the evening, we said our goodnights and retired into Drex's bedroom. He immediately stripped of his vest and pants. Silk boxers draped over his lower half, giving him plenty of breathing room, and me very little as he towered behind me.

Unable to get out of my fancy dress by myself, Drex undid the ties in the back. The dress fell loose, baring my breasts which were swiftly cupped from behind. He admired their freed heaviness. As I kicked off the skirts, his hands massaged my shoulders and neck before guiding me to Drex's bed. I hadn't yet put on my night clothes. I was in my panties. Drex would be my personal furnace. We got under the blanket and cuddled up. My body quickly sucked heat from his. He pulled me close, his arm brushing against my breast.

The day had left me exhausted, but also with an aching need for affection. I wanted to replace the grief with passion. I wanted to replace my insecurities with the security of his arms. I needed him to want me. I pressed my lace-covered ass against him, arching my back slightly with a sexy sigh.

It worked. I felt his cocks begin to grow behind me. Their heads tapped against my lower back. He tilted his head down and breathed hot, heavy air in my ear. I loved how quickly I turned him on, even after a busy day and Orkain encounter. Now just a handful of breasts and a laced ass had him propositioning me with our family and colleague just across the hall.

While I knew the rotha pair were probably tearing up my room having wild sex. I looked over my shoulder in mock surprise at his audacity.

His voice was rough and hushed. "You'll have to be a good girl and be quiet."

Shit. I liked his game.

I let out a soft whimper of compliance as his hand grabbed my hip and yanked me against him. I wanted him to do things to my body that would make me scream out, and then I wanted him to stop those screams.

I arched my back and pressed my ass against his crotch. He pressed back. Excitement rushed through me, settling as a rapid beat in my chest and as heat between my legs. I arched my back, taking my shoulders off his chest, and craning my neck so that he could look down and see my face as I pressed against his growing mass. He gave me a kiss on the forehead before tightening his grip around my breasts. His fingers found one of my nipples, and pinched and pulled it obscenely, sending sparks and wetting my panties. He grabbed my other breast with a playful roughness. It turned me on, and I desperately wanted his mouth on them—I wanted to feed them to his mouth full of tongues. But when I went to turn around, his strong arms tightened around me and held me in place. He breathed heavily into my ear; his face tight against mine. It was a subtle move, but I understood. He was in control, and he wanted me just like this.

His hand let go of my breast, brushed the other one just to appreciate it, before moving down my belly. His fingertips grazed my thighs as his palm passed over my panties. "You're so soft," he murmured. "But, are you wet yet?"

I gave a little whimper as his hand slipped inside my underwear. Intentionally skipping over my clit, he ran his fingers in a tingling arc of motion.

I moaned.

Correctively, he pulled the fingers from their petting and inserted them into my mouth to quiet me. I lapped with my tongue, tasting how turned on I was. A response bulged against my ass.

After his reminder, he returned to play with my pussy, swollen with heat and desire. A wet finger tracing invisible routes of pleasure along my body's map to his destination. With one finger stiff on my clit, he dashed another finger inside me, and I gushed into his hand, intensely wet.

As if they were their own creature, his cocks crept from their boxers and slithered into the waistband of my panties, pulling them down over the roundness of my ass. His hand assisted from the front. It was a move a human cock would never be able to pull off. The panties were soggy on my toes when I kicked them off.

The heads pulsed into my back momentarily before they snaked their way down, separating my ass cheeks, and slipping between my legs. A primordial fear took hold and adrenaline rushed through my body as the meat of my thighs was displaced to accommodate his large mass. All the while, he cooed for me to stay quiet for him.

He pressed against my folds, coating himself with my dew, brushing against my clit which was now on fire with desire. His top cock pressed on my asshole.

"You better stay quiet, my love," he growled before biting my ear.

His lower cock reached at a deep angle to stab at my clitoris as he sunk the other two into my channels. His hand came up to intercept my noises of surprise and pleasure. He pulled at my jaw as he strained in satisfaction.

I was full to the brim and needy at the same time. My teeth clamped onto the meaty part of his hand as his cocks pulled to the edges to immediately crash back into me. Again, and again. For a moment it was too much, and then I desperately needed more. I squirmed in his tight embrace as he smashed into me. I abandoned all thoughts as he reached deep into me, my channels clenching and holding him. His trunk pulsed, and fought for real estate as the one in my ass leaned into my main channel. He grunted with the effort of pulling himself in and out of my tightening body. The rod against my clit corkscrewed wildly against me, slapping my clit and setting me into a frenzy. Waves of pleasure set every cell in my body ablaze until my body clenched so tightly that Drex stopped thrusting and just let my channels grab him like a vice as I came. Cum leaked out of me, coating us with the liquid rush of my orgasm. My muscles tempered and relaxed. I'd left a bruise on his hand but I had been a good girl. I hadn't given anything away as I gave everything away.

He pulled out of me. Grabbing a towel from his bedside, he cleaned me up. He took good care of me. He hadn't orgasmed. I guessed it had been all for me. It worked. I was on a downhill coast into deep serenity. I would've offered him a blow job, but he promptly curled around me, intertwined cocks laying heavy and sticking to the back of my thighs. He breathed thick and comfortably in my ear until I fell asleep in his arms.

Chapter Twenty-Five
Try Again

Drex

Fortunately, there hadn't been any news about the Orkain taking off with anyone last night. It was already late morning. The dew had dried on the milcress. The blossoms of the flowers along the trail had retreated in advance of the bright sun. It would get warmer—and thus, safer—as the day went on. Neither Vance nor I expected to find anything as we scouted the route to his and Sara's home, but we did so anyway.

"You know, if we had an underground banquet hall, we could have *real* kumiratas. The whole village could come," piped up Vance as we watched the skies.

Vance had always been a huge proponent of creating a network of underground tunnels for protected travel. Unfortunately, it would require massive amounts of new construction, especially if it now included a banquet hall. I had been hesitant for many reasons. One, it felt like surrender—were we going to permanently give up the surface of Xavia to the Orkain? And second, it hadn't been the priority. What was the point of building infrastructure if our future was so uncertain? Sure, we had many young and spry men now, but who would maintain the tunnels?

"Or at least, Sara and I could have gone home last night and celebrated in our own way. I had made a few *special arrangements* for the night," he teased, lightly punching my shoulder.

"Then I wouldn't have been able to hear you and your lover all night," I said, happy to respond in a non-official manner.

"Sara is a screamer," he responded, nonplussed. "But I do need you to start thinking about the logistics of a tunnel system. I'm going to have a family. I need to be able to keep them safe. These tunnels should have already been done."

I guessed Vance was a step ahead of me. He would soon be with young, and he rightly worried they would be snatched up. Maybe he was right.

Perhaps I had been going about this all wrong. Katy would feel safer here if she could venture out by herself. How could I expect her to stay on a planet where she could easily become prey? I should have done so much more to prepare for her arrival. Perhaps then she would have at least fallen in love with the planet, if not with me. Or, at least she would have been more comfortable staying here. Besides, I would need a big program to keep me distracted when Katy left.

"We will make the next meeting about them. You are right."

"Wow, that's a first," he said.

We walked farther along the trail, looking out for the obvious signs in the sky. Vance was as lost in thought as I was, unfortunately, it ended up being about how to broach another topic.

"Do you think that you and Katy are rotha?" asked Vance. He tried to ask with nonchalance, but I knew otherwise. The nubs on his head were tight to the base of his horns. It was a look I was familiar with since we were children, and any time he disagreed with me now that we were leaders in our village.

"I'm not sure," I said, diplomatically. I hoped he'd accept that answer. Some of these things took time. And you didn't have to be rotha to be happy with someone, or importantly, to have babies. Sara and Vance were a wonderful miracle, but we didn't necessarily need miracles. We just needed babies.

"Is she not pleased with you?"

I swung my head and snarled. My eyes flashed with anger. He had meant it half-jokingly, but I made him regret it.

He backtracked. "I only ask because others are having issues—not you two, necessarily—or maybe you're not pleased with *her...*" he stumbled over his words, trying to return to his point.

It gave me time to recover. My quick-tempered reaction surprised even me. The hurt, anger, and fear had been bubbling close to the surface, and sprang when he touched on a possible truth. I'd been tensed. The kumirata and Vance's success didn't help for sure. Maybe I was jealous.

"Anyway, I wonder if we should offer our guests the opportunity to spend time with different hosts, if desired. We're approaching halfway through their stay, and we want everyone to have a good...experience," he finished lamely.

"I am incredibly pleased with her. I'm not sure she is pleased with me," I admitted.

Give Katy the opportunity to get to know someone else in our village? The thought made me sick. Her rotha existing on Earth was one thing—a distant possibility for her forever-happiness. But selfishly, if anyone were to make her temporarily happy, I wanted it to be me. It had to be me.

"Her sister told me that she isn't over a past relationship on Earth," said Vance, carefully. "Sara hoped that spending time with you would help her heal."

So even Sara knew there were feelings that hadn't been broken. I hung my head, too ashamed to tell him of my own rotha. Why would the fates curse me like this?

"Katy has told me multiple times that she's only come here to make sure Sara is safe. You, unfortunately, have made that true. Sara appears wonderfully safe and happy. I fear that Katy will return to Earth when the time comes."

"So maybe you need to hand her off to another of our hosts. Maybe they can get her to change her mind," he said carefully, the nubs on his head practically riding his horns now. "And you could get someone else, and personally show them what a wonderful place this can be. I assume you are taking good care of them, correct? I couldn't hear you over the screams of my own lover." He smirked good-heartedly.

"She held my hand over her mouth. I pleased her." I showed him my hand which had small purple bruises from her teeth that dappled my green skin.

He gave me a playful and proud shove while shaking his head. "Perhaps she will be less likely to leave than you believe."

I nodded, but he didn't know the truth. He had rotha behind him, and I had rotha against me.

"I don't see any Orkain out here. I think it's time I get my mate home and please her again. You can do the same with yours." If anyone else had heard him talk like that, I would have been embarrassed. I actually still was, but I knew that he was relying on years of our camaraderie and, he had his rotha. That was what they did.

Maybe Vance was right. Stars, how many times had I said that in my life? Too many times to count. I had to think about what was best for the village. I needed to consider "trading" Katy for another, so that I and another host could have a second shot at keeping a human woman here to find a new life among us. We had to make the best of the opportunities given to us, and that had been thirty women dropped on our doorsteps. Still, it felt impossible to bear the thought of Katy being with another.

Chapter Twenty-Six
Lost Touch

Katy

It was getting close to lunchtime, so Sara helped me prepare a lunch for everyone, just in case there was a bad report and they had to stay longer. When Vance and Drex returned with good news, I invited them to stay anyway, but I think they were anxious to return to their home after being delayed. I shared one more giant hug with my sister. While she could sometimes be a pain, I was glad to have had some extra time with her.

Drex sat down at his usual seat and pulled it close to the small table. "I was going to make you lunch," he said, looking over the various dishes.

"I made you lunch instead," I said, settling down on the opposite side which had quickly become my usual spot. The other two chairs had made the table crowded, so I had pushed them away when I removed the extra setting places.

I didn't necessarily need a 'thank you,' but I wasn't sure how to take his comment. Sara and I had prepared sort of grazing plates, where everyone could get whatever snack food they wanted. There was fruit, vyg, and some strips of dried meat. Maybe he thought I was being wasteful? I sat, unsure. We had shared a hot moment last night, but I still felt raw with emotion. Sara had been so dismissive about my plans. And I was growing more and more uncomfortable not discussing them with Drex. On one hand, my plans hadn't changed, so it felt insulting to repeatedly announce I'd be leaving Xavia at first chance. But my reasons had changed. There were more layers to it now—layers I hoped he'd understand.

"Thank you," he said, waiting for me to serve myself first.

If I thought the 'thank you' was going to help, it did, but not as much as I would have hoped. Drex seemed lost in his thoughts as well. After I began serving myself, he started, putting plenty of meat and fruit on his plate, and not a lot of vegetables—like a lot of men I've known. I had a very small sample size, but maybe that was universal. He didn't eat any of it, though. He intertwined his fingers and rested his elbows on the table. His stare landed somewhere in the lost space between his hands and the food on his plate.

That's where his eyes remained as he spoke. "We are nearing the halfway point of when we think the Earth ship will return."

He had been thinking about plans, too.

He continued, "Vance suggested offering the opportunity for guests to switch hosts. While everyone is getting along, perhaps we can find more successful matches if we take the opportunity to re-arrange the populace. What do you think?"

My eyes widened in surprise. Did he not want me here? I thought we'd been getting along…but, wait, wasn't that what he just said? He needed more than people just getting along. He needed babies. Ugh. I was glad he wasn't looking at me. I took the moment to gather my thoughts. This wasn't about me. I needed to be careful about this.

"It makes sense," I said slowly. "The whole point of the Xavians agreeing to this program was to make babies. Why send us back without trying at least one other host that might spark rotha or at least another baby or two?" After a pause, I added my question. "Would we switch?"

He looked at me, uneasy, unsure. That gave me his answer already. He asked a question, instead, "Are you still leaving with the next Earth ship?"

"Yes," I said quicker than I intended.

His eyes clouded with pain, but I didn't know if it was because he was hurt, or because he didn't want to hurt me. I took a deep breath. I liked Drex. I didn't want to meet anybody else. But I was going to leave anyway, right? I was making a practical decision, so how could I blame him for doing the same? And, on the other side of liking Drex, I wanted him to be happy. I wanted him to have what his best friend Vance had with my sister. I wanted him to be with someone who truly made him happy and gave him lots of babies. He deserved it. More than anyone I knew, he deserved it. He was under all of this pressure to not just lead his village, but to try to save it from extinction. He deserved to be with someone who made at least some part of his life tolerable. I couldn't stand in the way of that. Easily one of the other women would be able to see these wonderful qualities in Drex. Thoughts of another woman sharing his bed, relishing in his intense and fiery touch invaded my mind. I'd enjoyed last night's romp, cuddling, and sleeping with him.

However, maybe he hadn't orgasmed because he hadn't wanted to with me. Maybe he was just pleasing me out of an obligation as the prince—perhaps he'd be happier with another.

While I'd been eager to explain my reasons for leaving at the start of the meal, the information now felt insignificant—excuses in the face of nobler causes. However, if he was going the practical route, I would definitely stay my course, too. "I only agreed to come here for two reasons. The first was to make sure my sister was safe. She is. My second reason was financial, for which I need to return to Earth to make use of that."

He blinked, and the knobs on his face rose. "Financial?"

"Uh, yes, I was paid to come. I needed the money," We hadn't discussed the particular aspect in the light of the sex-trafficking. But, of course, they offered me money. It's not like I could afford this interstellar trip out of pocket.

His face fell as he thought it over. He was probably thinking about what financial incentive would be required to convince us women to stay and be their baby-mamas. He had to think about his people; I had to think of myself. Someone had to. And I hadn't in so long.

"If you are planning to leave, then I guess, if you are willing, we can put ourselves in the pool to switch. I owe it to my people to find a match. And perhaps someone else can change your mind about leaving."

So that's what all of this was about? Was I just a means to an end? And since it wasn't working out, now we were going to musical-chair switch partners? At the same time, his people were at stake. It didn't seem like something I had the right to refuse, so that I could remain comfortable for six months.

I felt the heavy silence sitting between us like some insurmountable chasm. With each moment that passed where we chose not to speak up, I wondered if the bridge between us was deteriorating. It wasn't how I had planned lunch, but I was sort of glad that it had all come out now. It would make the actual departure day that much easier. I could focus on my sister. Making sure she had everything she needed. I could tie up any loose ends that she had on Earth. Heck, she had made me beneficiary if she didn't return to Earth or upon her death. I was going to be in good shape when I got back. It would give me plenty of time to figure out a new job and everything. It was easier to think about those things, rather than being dumped by Drex.

I had promised myself I was going to make practical decisions, because before I hadn't and that had led me to being left at the altar. Men leave. It was apparently universal, just like the meat-eating. He couldn't even wait for me to go home. Obviously, I was making the right decision here. Still, it stung.

"Thank you for being such a wonderful host. I'm sure your next guest will be able to appreciate it. I hope you find rotha," I said. I picked up my plate of uneaten food, muttered something about eating in my room, and left the table for him to clean. If he had felt so obligated to please, he could deal with it as I prepared for another ridiculous life-change. Also, I didn't want him to see me cry.

Random interactions popped into my mind and played like a film for review. Would he have kissed anyone else that sweetly? Was he going to watch my favorite television show with someone else? I thought we'd connected, but it also wasn't the first time I'd thought something stupid like that. I hated the thought of him being with another woman. It made me feel sick in my stomach. But that wasn't something I could control. There'd been so little I controlled. My government—full of men—had dumped me here, and Drex had been so freaking handsome. I had never had someone care for me like that…ever. My fiancé hadn't even treated me that well. But I guess that's what I get for falling for him. He was just like all the other men in my life. Now, my escape plan was my only safe thing—the only thing I could rely on—in this world, and in the next.

I shoved my face into a pillow from the too-big chair by the vanity and screamed into it. It was the second time I had muffled my screams in the last twelve hours, but now tears crowded the edges of my eyes as I felt my heart break.

Chapter Twenty-Seven
Torn

Drex

Katy departed from the table with her plate, leaving me stunned. "Thank you for being such a wonderful host. I'm sure your next guest will be able to appreciate it. I hope you find rotha," she had said.

"I hope you find rotha."

My heart twisted in my chest when my destined mate said those words to me. She couldn't tell I experienced rotha already *with her*. Everything that I had been working toward, that I thought maybe *we* were working toward was thrown away with those words. Maybe she didn't feel anything for me.

I munched on a particularly dry piece of jerky. She already seemed tense when I mentioned lunch. She was really against me making her food. She always acted like she would owe me something if I did something for her.

I felt obligated to tell her what Vance had suggested about the Switching Day, but I didn't think she would actually go for it. I thought she was comfortable here! I thought we had *some* chemistry, but maybe I was blinded by rotha. She wasn't even comfortable with me making her lunch. A man was supposed to care for his woman, but she seemed to resent it.

I didn't want to keep her if she didn't want to stay. I thought I was doing an okay job. Wasn't she crying out in pleasure? Didn't she cuddle me on the couch while we watched those confusing TV shows from her planet? And I had given her what she had wanted—a job.

Fryyre—that had surprised me. She was getting paid, apparently a lot, to visit. I tried to reconcile her desire for money with what I knew about her.

Now the job here made sense. She'd told me that her job on Earth hadn't been ideal, but now she would be better situated. Unable to work because of her struggles with rotha, she'd come all the way out here in an attempt to make money. And what did she care about after her sister? She wanted a job. Was she expecting to get paid? She hadn't said so, but that seemed to be her goal. She had been so adamant. I had thought it was simply because she didn't want to feel obligated to me, but now I knew there was an entire world and future she was preparing for—and I wasn't going to be included in it. She hadn't come to this planet to be with me; I was finally realizing that wasn't going to change. I hadn't understood her, or us, at all. She was alien, but so precious to me. I wanted her to have everything she wished, so I wasn't going to stop her departure for Earth or even for another Xavian if that's what she wanted.

The jerky sat as a lump in my cheek. I forced it down, then cleaned up the table. At least she had left that for me to do. I wrapped the food in waxed fabric, and stored it. Perhaps I would be hungry for dinner.

Anger simmered and I slammed my hand on the slate counter. I hated my obligations. In another world, I'd fight for my mate, wait eons for my mate. I would figure out how and why she could be experiencing rotha with someone else, and I would find a way to interrupt it. Unfortunately, I didn't have that luxury. Instead, I needed to see if someone else would accept me as a mate. Objectively, even if Katy wasn't attached to someone on Earth and I hadn't been successful with her, I owed it to my people to offer her all the opportunities to find happiness here. Maybe she'd fall in love with someone else and stay on Xavia. It clearly wasn't going to be with me. That broke my heart. I would be hosting a new woman with a broken heart.

Perhaps that's how Katy felt. No wonder she didn't want me to do things for her. Tasks were easy compared to conjuring feelings that weren't there. My heart broke even more. Katy was doing her very best, and here I was a dope, still trying to get her to want me in the most desperate and foolish ways.

I didn't know what to do. Katy had said humans drank alcohol to feel better, but fage didn't work that way. It could only grow happiness already planted. It did nothing if you were in a bad mood. I found myself continuously glancing at Katy's door, hoping that she would come out and tell me she had changed her mind about switching, that she wanted to stay with me. I couldn't believe she would rather take her chances with another than stay here with me. It's not like anyone in the pool was bad. I personally vetted them. It's just, I thought she liked me…at least tolerated me.

And worse, I had to plan the whole thing.

I'd ask Sara to address the women and encourage them to switch hosts if they thought their situation could be improved. She could extol the greatness of rotha romance and encourage them to take another leap.

I drafted my announcement to the hosts. While we celebrated the fating of Vance and Sara, I didn't want them to think that was the only option. I would tell them of my surprise, the possible rarity, and that I knew of no others. (That last part was obviously a lie.) To switch or continue to host the same person would be a personal choice. If one party wasn't happy, they owed it to themselves to try again. It wouldn't be anything against them. I'd tell them Katy and myself would be back in the pool; there was no shame in it.

It wasn't just the Xavians I needed to convince that rotha wasn't the only option. I needed to convince myself.

I wrote my speech and sent it to Vance and Davian for feedback. I requested Sara's help with the women. It wasn't until I'd sent the transmissions that I realized it was only the day after their kumirata…after they had already had to spend the night here. I sent another hurried message that they should spend time celebrating.

Vance replied good-heartedly. He realized it was important and they would work on it "in between." Sara said she would be honored to address the women, and that she'd check on Katy. I guessed she already knew of Katy's plans.

#

"Switching Day will take place in two weeks. Submission deadline will be next week. Please submit your individual answer of *Stay* or *Go*. If you have any requests or preferences, we will match you appropriately. All of your answers are confidential."

The responses to Switching Day came swiftly. Vance and Sara stayed. Several other couples submitted *Stays* immediately. One couple immediately said *Go*, both parties involved. I avoided reviewing the paperwork. I didn't want to imagine hosting whoever the woman was…and more importantly, whoever Katy would be matched with. The thought of her with another man set my entire being on fire, and not in a good way. I had it within me to physically destroy anyone who would touch Katy. I'd have to calm myself before the Switch.

Some of the shame had passed, but the failure and heartbreak remained. All of my zarata shouted to not let her go, but what was I supposed to do about it? It was out of my hands. Even if I said no, Katy would say yes, and we'd both be in the pool.

Katy was my rotha; I had to focus on her needs and wants, and not the part that encouraged me to abscond with her to somewhere where neither of us had obligations. I couldn't be selfish, even if my only desires were to shower her with riches and affection, to please her every moment of the day, and to have her scream my name at night. She would be mine. She would settle this pain inside my heart that cried out for her, or if not, death.

It could not be death. I had my people to care for.

My heart was torn. I needed my lover, but she was not mine.

Chapter Twenty-Eight
Switching Day

Drex

As I did for their arrival, I wore a long linen shirt and regalia pants. They would serve me well for moving guest belongings in the sun today. Matches were being announced. While there were few benefits to leading such a small village—at least there wasn't a lot of room for fancy crap.

Vance and Sara had chosen the new host-guest pairs. I hadn't trusted myself to be objective when it came to Katy's match, so I had them do it. Purposeful coordination would have been done from the start, but the Orkain encounter had distributed us organically. Every man in the pool had grabbed a woman and taken her home. It was barbaric and rudimentary, but it had worked surprisingly well. Vance and Sara were a success. It had worked for me. In an emergency, our hearts had followed our fates. We had never done anything like matchmaking before. Rotha hadn't given up on us. Vance and Sara were proof-positive that a Xavian and a human could experience rotha. They were proof that rotha was still here to help us push through this tragedy. We would fight, strive, and thrive with the next generation to come where rotha was on our side. And that was a hope to keep.

At this point, I was ready to fly to Earth and murder the human who had broken Katy's heart, because he was the direct cause of my heartbreak. He didn't deserve her. He didn't deserve to be anywhere near her. The fates were cruel. The forces world wanted us alive, but separate. I'd rather they just swallowed me up incarnate, and be done with it.

Katy stepped out wearing a large tan striped shirt-dress she had cinched at the waist which showed off her figure. She had braided her hair so that it didn't fall into her beautiful face. She had gained some freckles on her nose and on her cheeks; I guess they had faded during her time in stasis. I was glad I hadn't kept her too underground. Part of my job in these trying times was to convince people to come out of their houses; the sun was important not just for freckles but for our health. It wasn't good to be underground all the time when one wasn't used to it. We weren't cave rodents. We weren't worms. Even if the Orkain had pushed us underground. We needed sunlight and stimulation and outside interaction with our community.

Katy lugged two bags on her shoulders, the ones from her trip to the ship, and they were stuffed full. My heart felt as heavy as those bags looked. I rushed over to help her. She surprised me when she willingly parted with the bags. She seemed to decline any offer of help when possible. The bags were heavy. Everything within me wanted to march them straight back to her room, but instead I dropped them at the door and watched them slump like my hopes.

"Is that everything?" I said, without anything else to say.

"I think so. If not, I won't be far," she said with a weak smile. It was a precursor to being unreachable, across the skies, in a world that had no knowledge of my rotha. She would never know I held a lifetime of love and passion for her. Could I let her like that?

Fryyre, she was beautiful, such a timid thing. Once again, I burned with the thought of her wrapped up in the arms of *Mike* or one of my men. The fates hated me. I'd been cursed. I had been cursed to watch my people die. I had been cursed to watch my beloved share fates with someone else. I had to behave though. I would be no help as a mad king.

As I was convinced she was my only one and no one else would do—the better I understood her own fating. Everyone understood it—her sister, Vance. She had brought this so-called 'luggage,' and seemed dedicated to leaving with it. And I understood. Because I would do it too. I would do it in a heartbeat. The moment I knew my weakness, I knew hers.

Even more confusing, she wrapped her arms around me and gave me a big hug. My body instantly responded to hers. My heart sensed hers close and matched its slower beat. I smelled the scent wrapped in her hair, wafting with every subtle movement. I felt pained.

Another for me? The idea of anyone else left me unfeeling and numb. It did absolutely nothing for me. It was both flavorless and outrageous. I already knew, it would be her or no one. I'd made a terrible mistake entangling myself with Katy. I could blame duty, but honestly, I would gladly do it again. Not just in throes of ecstasy, this woman—in every moment we'd shared—had become everything to me.

"Thank you," she said.

"Of course. I wish you'd let me take the luggage from your room. They are too heavy."

She arched her neck to look at me. "They are not. Although, yes, I will gladly have someone help me carry them to my new home." My face contorted at the words. "But that's not why I'm saying 'thank you.' Thank you for being such a wonderful host. I was angry, but mostly scared when I arrived on this planet. You saved me from the Orkain, and then you gave me a home, a wonderful home. Everything I know about this planet is thanks to you. You opened up and showed me your world. I am forever grateful for that."

"I hoped it would eventually be your world, but I understand…" I spoke. I lowered my head down and nuzzled my forehead with the top of her head, releasing her sweet scent and letting it swirl around my own head. I closed my eyes and realized *this* was my world. She was my world. And I was losing it.

The settit made noise and interrupted the moment. It was Vance.

It was my demise.

"Haellea Prince, haellea Katy," he greeted us. He was wearing some fancier official garb. He didn't need to move belongings. He had what he wanted, and his smirk said as much. I hated him in that moment, but I also knew it would pass. It was jealousy. It was my rotha crying out for a scenario that wasn't mine.

"I want you to know that Sara and I worked on the matches, and we did it two ways. One with you and Katy in the pool, and one without."

"I don't think that's necessary," I said quickly, afraid to even think about it. Afraid that Katy would be offended.

"It actually is, because, you see. We counseled all of the other couples, but we didn't counsel you two. It is important that we follow protocol here. I'm going to get off the settit and let you two talk it over."

So much for 'counseling' and protocol. He was giving us a way out. He was giving us a second chance.

"Maybe this is for the best, you know?" she said almost immediately, like she didn't want or need a moment to think about it, like she wanted to say that first before anything else was said.

"How so?"

I had to tell her.

I had to tell her.

I had to tell her.

I believed in rotha. My parents were rotha partners. It was this magical, powerful thing that tied them. If she was trying to leave, then this wasn't it. It couldn't be it. The fates had gotten it wrong. Maybe a mix-up regarding the species and the planets. Maybe the stars got crossed on the way over, but this couldn't be the magical undeniable force that bound my parents. If she wanted to leave. She could leave.

I wasn't going to stop her.

"I'm leaving for Earth in just this same amount of time. It's best for both of us to get some distance. You are such a good host. I know that your next guest will be just as smitten as I am. It is what's good for your people. And spending time apart before I leave is what's good for me."

I would give her whatever she wanted, even if it killed me. It felt like it was killing me.

"I will have you back in a heartbeat," I said. I've never had such a wonderful time with someone. You are incredible. Please come back if it's not the same elsewhere…anywhere."

She nodded with tears in her eyes, and I could tell that she knew that I wasn't just talking about her new host's home, but her home planet. And the fact that she was still ready to walk out this door, told me she felt this way about someone else. She had to, right?

She gave me a kiss, an open-mouth, dry but intense kiss that was a farewell and a heartbreak all in one moment.

She pulled away, nearly trembling.

Why wouldn't she stay?

"Please call Vance back," she said quietly as she walked away and busied herself with her bags.

So, I did.

Vance sighed and folded the sheet he held and replaced it with another. Katy returned. I waited nervously to know who Katy would be matched to. I didn't much care about mine. It didn't matter. I would be respectful and take care of them, but it wasn't like I was going to find my rotha. Mine was right here, in this very room. She was close enough to touch, but she seemed lightyears away already. I would cross that distance if I knew how.

I steeled myself to hear the name of the man that might be able to do what I could not.

"Katy will be matched with Chelk."

Chelk. My upper lip opened into a snarl involuntarily but thankfully no noise had escaped. Chelk was a soldier, of 'good stock,' but I didn't care for him particularly. He was all muscle and no finesse. Katy praised my muscles and body though, so she would enjoy his even more. The pit in my stomach grew vacuous. It threatened to swallow me up.

"Drex?" asked Vance.

I forced myself to come back into focus. I managed a nod. I was becoming more human by the day.

"Do you want to know who you are matched to?"

"Layla."

I didn't know much about Layla. She hadn't been Chelk's partner who had shared some loud arguments. I hadn't heard anything about Layla and her match. To be honest, I couldn't even remember which one she was matched to. I didn't really care.

We received our schedule to move Katy. Everything was in staggered stages for safety. There was nothing else to do besides hang up with them and wait.

"Tell me about Chelk," Katy requested from the urish. Her feet were curled underneath her, her arms wrapped around her legs, in a small, fearful ball. Every cell in my body cried out to comfort her. I moved to her and put my arms around her.

She straightened inside my embrace, feigning a cough to distance me. She would gather her courage without me.

"He's a soldier in our army against the Orkain. He's mid-ranking. He surpassed all of our physical requirements. He satisfied intellectual and emotional testing." I spouted off facts, rather than share a thoughtful opinion.

"So, he's a meathead?" she asked.

"A 'meathead'?"

"Just all muscle and no brains. Just meat up there too," she said with a giggle.

"Ah yes, that's perfect. A meathead."

"Maybe don't call him that to his face. It's not a very nice Earth term," she said quickly.

"I don't think he would understand it," I said. We both laughed.

The humor broke some of the ice building. We were united for a moment. I even felt better about her given match. She was going to hang out with a meathead. I hoped she would find him intolerable. Chelk wouldn't understand her need for a job—I barely did. They wouldn't be able to converse on the same level. Perhaps that was Vance's intention.

Chapter Twenty-Nine
The Drop Off

Katy

Drex had the unfortunate task of moving me and my few belongings to Chelk's home. Our trek was silent. I didn't have any comforting words, and I knew he couldn't give me what I wanted. This was the best that we could do.

I wasn't sure if I could handle this breakup, but focusing on my tasks, packing, and planning had helped. Last time, I didn't have plans or an escape route. This time I had a plan. I took care of myself. And that didn't necessarily make me feel entirely good, but it helped. I had protected myself. It had been the smart thing to do.

Chelk was at the door when we arrived. My first impression echoed Drex's description—hulking, and somewhat vacuous. He was taller than Drex, and as broad-shouldered as Vance. His turquoise skin had a sheen. He was missing part of a horn. The edges were jagged but appeared softened with oil. The nubs along his head were almost invisible. I might not have noticed them if they hadn't become familiar to me during my time with Drex. It made his face look broad, and his eyes were dull, not like the spinning galaxies I saw in Drex's eyes.

Drex shrugged off Chelk's offer and carried my bags through the house. Chelk obliged—pointing out which room to put them in—but ground his teeth. Then he turned his sights on me.

"Hello, Katy. I take it you didn't like the prince," he grinned. It was a bold way to start a conversation.

"I liked him fine." He caught me off guard, as did my response. I hadn't meant to use past-tense.

His house was familiarly schemed, a smaller version of Drex's house. His settit sat in the living room rather than an office; it was half-sized, like the one I had in my room. Obviously Chelk didn't need an office, but I would miss talking to my sister in private.

Drex re-entered the living space and surveyed the room, as if it required his approval. I was secretly glad that Drex was throwing his weight around. I wanted Chelk to think twice about any sort of romance that he thought might be upcoming. I wasn't ready or willing. I wasn't sure what his previous experience was with his first guest, or what he thought would come of us.

I'd always assumed my attraction to Drex had to do with his amazing body—a body that could be found in magazines, not in real life. For all intents and purposes, Chelk had a nice body—maybe even nicer than Drex's—but I felt absolutely no attraction to him, whatsoever. I already knew I would be fine leaving this man's house to go back to Earth in six months.

Before the awkward small talk could begin, I excused myself to wash the dust off my feet and legs from the walk. I could at least be a polite guest while I was staying here. I retrieved a couple of things from my bag before heading to the bathing room. I heard them speaking in angry hushed whispers as I stepped into the hallway.

Chelk had a plunge pool, but no body dryer or luxurious surrounding lounging space. What did I expect? Chelk wasn't a prince. I turned on the shower, knowing how to handle all the buttons now, and did a rinse of my feet. I found a towel and patted them dry.

I was already in the hallway before I realized the shadow over me. I let out a yip in surprise.

Chelk's laugh rattled in his chest. His large bulk took up most of the hall's width.

"I didn't mean to frighten you," he said.

"It's okay. I didn't expect you out here." I straightened, embarrassed. "Is Drex still here? I'd like to say goodbye." I peeked over his shoulder.

"No, the prince left," said Chelk. He turned his body to the side so I could see into the empty living room.

I actually surveyed the empty room, not because I didn't believe Chelk, but because I couldn't believe Drex had left without saying goodbye. He didn't check to make sure I was doing OK, or if I needed anything? That man had constantly checked on me since I set foot on the planet. Not anymore, I guessed.

"Are you hungry?" Chelk asked.

I couldn't process if I was hungry. I defaulted to a list of excuses and hoped one of them would catch— whatever landed me safely in my room to work out what had just happened. Had Drex really left me?

"I'm not hungry yet, thank you. I hope you understand I am very tired from this travel and the stress of Switching Day. I'm sure you are too."

"Sure, I understand," he said.

I slipped apologetically into my room, closing the door even as he remained in the hall. I felt bad; I wasn't usually that rude.

My hand reached for the deadbolt but only found scuffs on the wood where it'd been evidently removed; I locked the handle. I put my back against the door and sank to the ground to sort out my thoughts.

The room and furniture were similar to my space at Drex's, but it was not mine. It didn't have the same little touches. There were no soft fabrics, curtains, or extra pillows. There was no small settit, like Drex had given me when he realized I would want to talk to my sister more often and more privately than his office could accommodate. Maybe Chelk wasn't as rich as Drex, but no personal touches showed Chelk hadn't put any thought into the room, over what had been provided for the hosting program. Drex had done extra, but I had to remember; it would have been for anyone. And now he had Layla. Tears in my eyes started to well up. What had I done? Why had I traded for this mystery situation? Because I couldn't handle my feelings for Drex? Because I was afraid that I was going to hurt when I left?

Well, guess what, Katy? You left and now you freaking hurt, I chided myself.

The tears streamed from my eyes, thankfully silently at first. It gave me time to crawl to the bed—the only place to muffle my crying. I didn't want Chelk to hear and feel obligated to investigate. I didn't want my first real experience with him to be one of tears. Truthfully, I didn't want any interaction with him. The bed was of familiar comfortableness. I sunk my head into the one pillow and let the grief finally hit me. It felt like a ton of bricks on top of me, threatening to suffocate me.

I sobbed until I felt like I was hyperventilating. I did *not* want to pass out or have a panic attack in a stranger's house. I pulled my head up and took gulping breaths. I had to talk myself down. I told myself it was good to cry now. I could get over it before getting into the stasis pod…ah, hell. It would have been so much better to go into a stasis pod and fall asleep, and just not have to think about this. Why would I do this to myself?

I distracted myself by entertaining the idea of powering up the stasis pod and falling into thoughtless sleep. I had no idea how to operate the Arqal technology in reality, I wouldn't abandon my sister so quickly, but it slowed and gathered my thoughts all the same. My breaths became even, and I pulled out my video player. I would sink into the bed, covered in blankets, and zone out. Pretend I was on Earth, where things made sense, where things weren't alien, where I didn't have to live with male hosts because of what other males had said. I didn't have to worry about the future of the Xavian people. I hadn't been tasked to photograph their dying culture.

I started a different TV series than the one that Drex and I were watching. I remembered his opinions of each character in *Telefunctional*; it now colored the way I watched the episodes. Watching an alien series had probably been very confusing for Drex, but he had taken it in good stride. He'd suggested to Davian the media distribution so that all households—humans and Xavians—could experience it. He really cared for us, all of us. Meanwhile, I hadn't even heard Chelk's name before Switching Day.

I turned on the hospital drama show, *HighCare Medical,* which contained even more ridiculous scenarios than my life was playing out. I zoned out. I zoned out for hours and hours. I didn't recall sleeping, but I must have, right? The room darkened and lightened before I got the first knock on my door.

There wasn't a mirror or settit to confirm what I looked like, but I had to look like crap. I was still in my dusty dress which had now dirtied the bed. Ugly crying made my eyes swell and puff up. My hair was matted. I didn't want Chelk—or anyone for that matter—to see me.

He knocked again impatiently before leaving. I forgot for two more episodes then heard him knock again. I wondered how many times I could not answer before he would open the door and check on me.

"The prince said you like a morning meal. I'll leave it here in the hallway."

I should have thanked him, but I didn't want to start a conversation. I was still too numb. I didn't say anything at all.

I binged until I was in actual pain from holding my pee. When the coast seemed clear, I slipped out of the bedroom, almost tripping over the food and drink that lay cold on the floor. I avoided the mirrors while I peed for what seemed like forever, then I tiptoed back into my room and locked the door behind me. Buried in the blankets, I started the next season of *HighCare Medical*. The hunky Korean doctor had been abducted to treat the mobster's son—who also happened to be the doctor's love interest. I didn't feel much for it, but I watched it play out in the glow of the computer screen. There was another tearful sobbing before dinner time. My eyes had welled up again.

"Are you going to eat dinner with me?" He could see that the breakfast food was disturbed, so he knew

I was still alive at least. I considered what I might say to him before he added, "You're being very rude, you know?"

I decided to say nothing at all.

#

Another season of *HighCare Medical* was over, I guessed. I wasn't sure. The screen had gone black a while ago. I sat staring at the dark screen. I remembered how this felt just a year or so ago—it was difficult to wrap my mind around how much time had passed—after the breakup, I'd disappeared in a hole for months. I had food delivered. My sister only saw me when she had managed to force her way inside.

When I returned to Earth, I wouldn't even have my sister to interrupt my grief. With the money I made, I could float in the sadness-abyss for as long as I needed. No one would bother me because they'd forget I came back.

Honestly, I couldn't remember my reasons for going back to Earth. I was ready to throw them all away in this wave of grief. It threatened to bowl me over even here. Would being an entire galaxy away from my sister and Drex actually help me?

I sniffed and sat up, wrapping my arms around my legs, wiping my face on the blanket. I knew this grief. I knew this pain. I thought I had made the right choice. I chose practicality and what was best for me…didn't I? Except… maybe I hadn't. Maybe I wasn't picking practicality, but instead I was picking pain and grief. Why when given the same choice, would I elect the one that hurt me so much? Did I think I deserved this? Was this the life I wanted to lead?

The question was a thick dagger in my chest I couldn't ignore. I wrapped my hands around the hilt. I hadn't done anything wrong on Earth. I had gotten dealt bad cards. But on Xavia, I had been dealt wonderful cards. I was given Drex. He respected and provided for me even when my needs were unexpected or confusing. He gave me a job, gave me purpose, and a kind ear. Why did I think he'd leave me as Mike had? He was not only an entirely different person. This was an entirely different planet.

I had thrown it all away because I feared the pain I *could* experience; well, that pain was here and now. I had chosen it. Drex had only ever given me whatever I asked for; agreed to everything I said. Perhaps he hadn't been trying to get rid of me. Perhaps he had wanted me to stay, but allowed me to leave.

At this point, if things didn't work out between me and Drex…if he left me, or I left him…then this pain would be here. It would be right here. Easily accessible. I had found it with one decision and two nights. I didn't need to choose it. I didn't need to pick it. I didn't need to embrace it. I experienced it. I knew its realness.

But it was time to choose something else. It was time to take a risk to *not* feel like this, to find someone and let them care for me. And I wanted to care for him. I loved his thoughtful gentleness, and his manly roughness. He was a wonderful mixture of everything I needed. I wanted to be with him. I wanted to be his guest and I wanted to stay even when given the opportunity to go back to Earth.

I wanted to be there for Drex and his people. I would never be able to contribute this greatly anywhere else. I wanted to help the Prince of Xavia. I wanted this group of people and their culture to continue. I wanted to live in it. I was in love with it. I was in love with Drex. I wanted to be here forever. Now that I was saying it to myself, I absolutely knew it was true.

I loved him.

This here, being in a stranger's room was a mistake. I needed to go see my love. I needed to let him know. Chelk was already displeased with me. I would not be able to do anything he didn't want me to do, if he knew. He was so much larger than me. I shouldn't have been so rude. I couldn't risk him stopping me. I needed Drex to know that I chose him. I chose love. I chose him. He was my fate, no matter how that fate turned.

Chapter Thirty
Lost

Drex

The settit sounded in my office and I groggily rushed out of bed. I knew the settit in Katy's room would wake Layla, my new guest. I had intended Katy to take the settit with her as it had been a gift. I discovered she'd left it behind when I prepared the room for Layla. Speaking of, poor woman. I hadn't been good company, sulking around and now her sleep was disturbed.

Vance's stricken face snapped me awake. What was wrong? I asked immediately.

"Chelk called me. Katy is missing," he reported.

"What??!" I roared. If Layla hadn't woken up yet, she had now.

"He doesn't know what happened or how long she's been missing. She'd been in her room watching that television thing of hers."

"She wasn't having a good time there?" I asked.

"I'm not sure this is the right time, but no, it sounds like she was miserable. She wasn't eating. He hadn't seen her since you left, basically."

As worried as I was, part of me was happy she hadn't been enjoying the new arrangement, or her new host. I was done talking. I'd been a wreck without Katy. My heart literally ached for her. I had to find her before something happened to her. She was so stubborn—demanding work, switching hosts, not taking her settit. I kicked myself. The tunnel system would absolutely have to be built, if only to save myself this pain.

As I put on my wrap sandals, Layla appeared in the doorway. Concern washed over her. "You'll find her," she assured me. She shoved a canteen of water into my arms as I rushed out the door.

The moons lined up over a star-swept sky, lighting the path before me. Before I could thank the fates, a shadow moved in my peripheral. I ducked to the jungle's edge.

Orkain.

Terror struck my heart. The Orkain were hunting tonight. It couldn't get any worse…I prayed the fates didn't have anything worse.

#

I arrived at Chelk's in record time. I knocked on the door and was shocked when he answered. I wanted to swing at him. I got in his face. Why was he inside when Katy was not? I shoved my way inside.

"What happened? What did you do to her?" I growled.

"Me?! What did *you* do to her? She's been hiding ever since you dropped her off. You care? You didn't even say bye to her."

I had stayed just long enough to make sure she'd have the things she needed and that he understood Katy was to be given the utmost respect in every matter. Katy would have complete control of any situation. She was the guest, and he was hosting her. She was not to entertain him. Then I had left quickly, because if I stayed longer, all the pain bubbling at the edges of my chest would explode. I'd see red and I'd pound Meat Man into the ground for even being near my love, Katy. I hated it. I hated every moment of it.

He reluctantly let me search the place. We were both seething. The bedroom still had her things packed. On the bed, she'd built a familiar nest of blankets in front of her video player. She was nowhere to be found.

"When do you think she left? When did you last hear her?" I demanded.

"The morning food I prepared *under your advisement*," he said with an angry tone, "had been knocked over. I replaced it with dinner. I thought I heard her after that, but dinner's not been touched."

So, the man had no idea.

I marched outside and used a torch light to investigate the area outside her window. It was useless. I wasn't a tracker. I couldn't tell if she'd taken the window. She could've taken the door when he was distracted. Either way, she was gone.

"Could the Orkain have taken her?" asked Chelk, examining the window.

I wanted Chelk to worry, and understand the depth of danger my love was in. But I needed to be honest. It was time for me to admit that she'd left on her own accord. "No, she's run off. She's done it before."

My anger was misplaced. I was to blame. I should have told her how I felt about her. I should have never let her leave. She would've been safe with me. I had to find her.

Katy didn't know how to get to Vance's and Sara's place from Chelk's. Her plan had to have been to retrace her steps back to my place, but she'd gotten off track, because I hadn't come across her. It would have been difficult. Even with the bright moonlight, everything looked different at night. And we still had few signs.

I thought back to the first night I'd lost Katy. She tried to follow the paths but had gotten lost. She was better at the paths now, so I retraced the path from Chelk's house and looked for places where she might've gotten confused and taken the wrong way.

The howls of the Orkain filled the night sky. The only thought that kept me from rushing around the forest like a madman screaming for her, was that the Orkain were *still* out hunting. They hadn't found her yet; else, they'd have retired for the night. And thank the stars, the moons were out to aid our search.

I had to find her before the Orkain did. I quickened my step, staying on the edge, trying to figure where Katy might've gone astray. Occasionally I chanced a few calls of her name, but mostly I searched the jungle with my eyes, my ears, and my zarata for whatever sign rotha might provide. By quieting my mind like I did in the mornings, I pulled strength from my zarata. It was clear to me now that I was fated to my love, and as much as I had been trying to disregard it, it was powerful. It hadn't been wrong with my parents. It had never been wrong in any story ever told to me. I was not the exception.

Katy and her ex were not rotha. I had a dull ache in my chest ever since I'd left her at Chelk's. It had intensified as I walked farther from her yesterday.

There was no way her ex would have been able to stay away this long if he had been destined for her. And she wouldn't have been able to leave Earth if she had been destined to him. I had faith in that now. She came to be with me. She hadn't known it then. Neither had I, but rotha had. She would understand and know eventually. Until then, I had to trust.

I took a fork in the road which was the wrong direction if one was going to my house. But as I walked that way, the ache in my chest got stronger. I listened. I turned back and took the fork toward my place. Perhaps she had gotten off track farther down. Every few steps, I closed my eyes and listened to my rotha heart. I wasn't perfectly in tune, but I could tell when I getting off course. I honed in on my love. I would find her.

Chapter Thirty-One
The Orkain

Drex

Soon, I was going off the trail into the jungle. It was dangerous to do so. The dense forest canopy made it a lot darker, and I could get lost just as Katy had. I couldn't see Orkain shadows either, only hear their flapping of wings and their howls overhead as they communicated their own search. It took everything in me to stay calm in those moments and focus on the one signal I could follow with my heart, my rotha.

A sharp, sudden pain in my chest wheeled me around. It was the same pain I'd gotten when I was first intimate with Katy. My eyes searched the darkness. She was nearby. I knew it.

So did the Orkain. Renewed fear gripped me as talons and wings swooped over me. It screamed. I eyed some brush to dive into for cover, but it wasn't after me.

It was after someone else.

Even in the darkness, I could make out the tiny shadowy figure as my love. I would not see her taken from me. Not by her government in a spaceship, not by her fears or my own, and definitely not by this primitive, flapping beast.

I launched myself as the beast slowed to grab Katy, not wanting to bowl her over. I landed, just barely, on the Orkain's back. I clambered higher, grabbing the crook of its wing, and finding purchase with my feet. I pulled my dagger from its sheath and sunk it where its wing joined its back. Warm blood covered my hand. The beast jerked, its back arching obscenely. Its bloodcurdling scream pierced my ears. I dug my blade farther, riding the beast, gripping with my legs as it bucked and rolled. I could hear Katy's terrified screams in the background. As long as I kept it busy, it couldn't harm her. Yanking my dagger from the joint, I slammed it into the back of its neck, where its horned head met its birdlike body. It sank easily to the hilt, my hand deep in feathers and blood. It thrashed longer than I expected, a disgusting writhing motion overtaking its body until it lay mostly motionless on the ground.

"Drex?" came the voice of a fearful angel.

My heart sang, despite the adrenaline pulsing through my body.

I dismounted the dead beast, dropped my dagger, and ran to her. My bloody arms held her tightly.

"Drex," she said again, a whisper into my chest where I had her face pressed. She felt so warm, so soft. I could smell her scent over the metallic scent of blood, and it was heavenly. She was my gift from the stars.

"Before you get mad—" she mumbled through her tears. She raised her head so she could meet my eyes in the dim light. I could never be mad at her. "I promised to not run away from *you*. I started at Chelk's house this time."

Her joke surprised me wholly. Here we were in the dangerous jungle, covered in blood, with a dead Orkain at our feet—the FIRST dead Orkain, might I add—and she was making fun.

I laughed and nodded. She was right.

My heart thumped hard. It was difficult to distinguish it from the dull ache that had established itself when Katy had first come into my life. It was an ever-present ache and a need for her.

"I have so much to tell you," I said. Instead of telling her any of it, I put her at half-arm's length and gave her a kiss. Her lips were soft and sweet; I forgot all about the pain and fear. Our lips parted too soon.

"I have things to tell you, too—" she started.

I pulled her into a hug and whispered in her ear. "Not here." Not in the dark with Orkain around us. They could have heard their comrade.

She nodded.

"We must get the rest of your search party back inside. It's not safe for them."

She gave me one more constricting hug. That sharp pain in my chest didn't return.

I found my dagger discarded in the dead leaves, and cleaned it on one of the beast's wings before plucking one of its long flight feathers. I tucked it and my dagger into my belt. I then took my love by the hand and led her back to our home. I was not going to spend one more night away from her.

#

Layla's eyes widened with shock when Katy and I arrived covered in blood. When she realized it was not ours, she wrapped her arms around Katy. They had hardly met before, but she was welcoming and tended to her as I communicated with the rest of the search group.

Chelk was visibly relieved. He correctly feared for his life if she had been harmed. I sent him and Vance to retrieve the Orkain's body for study. It was the first we had killed. The flying beasts' undersides were armored and invulnerable. We'd never launched an attack above them before. I suspected anywhere feathered was assailable.

After, Layla sent us to the bathing room with hot mugs of fah retired for the night. She said she'd speak with Chelk in the morning to see if he'd agree to take her as a guest. Katy and I were both thankful for her understanding. Layla had a warm heart.

"You look terrifyingly awesome," Katy said behind closed doors.

I glanced at myself in the mirrored section of the wall. My hair was tangled in my horns; blood crusted along the edges of my muscles. I felt strong, but incomplete until I pulled her close. Despite her smile, I realized she was shivering, coming down from the panic we had endured.

I removed her dress, which I realized was the one she'd left in, and let down her hair. I undressed as well, setting aside the dagger and the feather which were still in my belt.

"I am so sorry." Her gaze kept on the feather. "I didn't think I'd get lost—"

I hushed her. I took her hand and led her to the shower where I could wash the blood off her and get her warm.

She breathed heavily, her bosom rising and falling in jagged heaves as she tried to tamp down the adrenaline that remained in her system, ready to fight.

In the sprays of the shower, she put her bare, shaking body against mine, and we stayed that way, skin-to-skin. I kissed her head and held her tight until she calmed. Then, I poured some soaff into my palm and worked it gently into her hair.

"I'm glad you found me," she said.

I hesitated, distracting myself with a bit of blood matted in her hair. After I picked it out, I maneuvered her to rinse her hair.

"Do you know *how* I found you?" I asked. She shook her head underneath my fingers as I worked the soaff from her strands.

I went quiet again. After the rinse, she squeezed the excess water from her hair. "How did you find me?" she asked softly.

Another sort of terror clenched my heart, but it was nothing compared to being without her. The words tumbled from my heart. "I'm fated to you. It made itself known the first time I tasted you, although I haven't allowed myself to believe it. You are my rotha, Katy. All of my being was made for you, to please you, to be with you. You can't go. You can't go back to Chelk, and you can't go back to Earth. If you do, I will follow you there. I will follow you anywhere. I'm done denying my love for you. Your presence has given my life meaning. You are my gift from the stars. You are my rotha."

The relief I felt in telling her those words was quickly overshadowed by my fear. Did she feel the same? *Could* she feel the same? No matter. I had finally spoken my truth. My fate was in her hands.

Katy

"I'm your rotha?" I asked in near disbelief. Why hadn't he told me sooner? Why had we switched during Switching Day? My heart leaped and bound. It lurched and sang. It was everything I hoped for but didn't dare wish for.

"You are. I didn't want to believe it, because you and your fiancé—"

"—ex-fiancé," I corrected, and wished to correct more than that.

"I know rotha. If he's rotha to you, I will surely be left behind. But I've decided it doesn't matter. I can't deny it. I can't deny myself. You're the reason my heart beats the way it does. You are changing my body, and I can't do anything but confess my love and my experience. No matter what happens next, I had to be true to myself. I have to be true to you."

His eyes reflected resignation and pain. Did he really think that I shared rotha with that jerk on Earth? I hadn't talked to Mike since he left me at that stupid altar, which I was so thankful for. Nothing else would have gotten me here to Drex. I had traveled the stars and found my own destiny. Not rotha, maybe. It wasn't biologically written on my arms, but it was my fate all the same.

I had to set things right.

"Do you know why I left Chelk's?" I asked, tracing the rivulets of water dripping down his chest with my fingertips.

It was his turn to shake his head. His face solemn. My body was warm again, and now my heart warmed.

"I was coming to see you. I couldn't wait a minute longer. I had to tell you that I made a mistake leaving. And I was making a mistake by thinking I was going to leave Xavia. I was only leaving because I was scared of what I had here and of losing it. There is *nothing* on Earth I want. There is only you that I want. I've never been happier anywhere or with anyone else. Is it a risk? Yes. Might I lose you? Yes. But I'm not going to lose you on purpose. I want you to be my fate."

His face went through as many emotions as my heart had gone through at his confession. He picked me up, and I wrapped my legs around his waist, encased in his arms.

"You're my everything," I roughly whispered as he pulled me into a long-winded, passionate kiss. His tongues swept mine. It felt like relief. It felt like love. I couldn't get enough of it. I was never going to say goodbye again.

"You're my everything," he said in return as our lips parted for a moment.

I had never felt so complete.

For all the scary things that might happen, they'd be less so with his arms around me. I was not going to live in fear over things that happened a galaxy away. This was here. This was Xavia. And this was my Xavian romance. I'd never had anything like it. Drex was amazing, and he found rotha with me.

And maybe in time, I would experience rotha to him, but it didn't matter. His rotha bounded him to me; I was his forever.

He kissed me again, and bit my bottom lip with a need that I felt travel down my spine and through my core. I pressed my breasts to his chest and squeezed my legs tighter, as the shower got a bit wetter.

I got lost in the ecstasy after that.

Chapter Thirty-Two
Aftermath

Katy

I spent the morning with Layla as Drex worked to reverse our switch. I was glad I hadn't seen Layla in passing on Switching Day. She was gorgeous with dark ringlets, big eyes, and beautiful skin. I would have been out of my mind thinking about her and Drex together. Thankfully it hadn't worked out that way. Layla had been so good to us last night, and her graciousness continued throughout the next day.

"You know, we were all surprised when you participated in Switching Day! Everyone was betting you'd be announcing your kumirata next." She said over a cup of fah as we sat on the urish. She was excited things were working out between Drex and me.

"Well, I guess everyone else could see what we weren't ready to admit," I said. And, I could say it with a smile on my face now.

"Is it true, that our appearance changes with rotha?" She wanted the low-down since I was Sara's sister.

"It is true. Sara has the same markings as Vance."

"Do you have any?" she asked, conspiratorially.

"Not yet, but I'm so happy with Drex. I don't care if they show up or not."

"My first host was nice, but honestly, I wasn't attracted to him." She lowered her voice, "he reminded me too much of my brother."

"Your brother was green?"

She burst out laughing.

Despite how it had turned out for me, I felt obligated to tell her. "It's not a requirement to romantically connect with your host. We never agreed to this."

"I know. But I guess our government was good at picking us out."

I grimaced. It hadn't been something I'd voiced out loud to Sara or Drex, but I suspected—and apparently, Layla did too—that besides our fertility, there'd been other criteria we'd been selected for…our circumstances, personalities, and histories had made us ideal for their experiment. And for better or worse, it was working.

Layla didn't push it. "What is Chelk like?" she asked.

"I didn't really give him a chance. Hopefully, he doesn't look like your brother, though."

Our laughter was interrupted by a knock on the door. Layla excused herself. It was Chelk with my things, here to retrieve Layla.

"You! You scared the shit out of me."

He must've learned that figure of speech from his first guest…at least, I hoped. He rocked back and forth in the doorway and I remembered my manners, inviting him inside. Now back with Drex, I saw Chelk in a different light. I felt bad for how I'd treated him. I owed him an apology.

"I'm sorry I was a horrible guest. I was going through a lot. I thought I knew my way back, and was going to have Drex call you when I showed up at his doorstep." Even my apology was embarrassing.

"Hey, I wish I had a woman cause that much trouble over me. I'm glad you're safe." He gave a short bow, incongruous with his giant body.

"I'm still sorry to have worried you. If it makes you feel any better, I ran away from Drex the first night too."

"The first night? That does sort of make me feel better." He rubbed his shoulder with his opposite hand, sheepishly.

For as brutish as his body and horns looked, he had some cute, puppy-like expressions. I wondered why his first relationship didn't work out.

"Layla is sweet. I think you will like her."

He sighed, his shoulders rising and falling in proportion with his height which made it look like a huge defeat. "I don't know. I've been rejected twice."

"That's not true. You never had a chance with me!"

"Thanks," he said, sad.

"No, no, that's not what I meant!" I smiled so he knew I wasn't trying to be mean.

He nodded.

"Just be yourself, relax. I think she'll appreciate that. She's in your same boat, y'know."

"Boat?"

"Rejected twice," I said, using his words.

"She didn't have a chance with Drex. They hardly had time—" Chelk understood my point.

"So be as nice to yourself as you are to her."

This time his bow was more relaxed.

He was going to be just fine.

#

I unpacked my belongings, sorting them into things to keep in Drex's and my bedroom, and things for the spare bedroom. I considered how it might be a nursery room one day.

That was right.

I mean, we hadn't talked about it yet, but it was the whole point of the program from his people's end. They were going to die out in a couple of generations without help. And these were now my people, too. If he was a prince, I guessed that made me some sort of leader as well. I'd have to ask. I laughed to myself. I hadn't thought about it before now. All I knew was that I wanted to make him as happy as he was making me.

A family hadn't been on my mind when I left Earth. These last six months had changed so much. Now that I felt safe and secure with Drex, I couldn't imagine *not* having a family with him. He would be an amazing father. He proved he'd do anything for our family when he let me go on Switching Day. He denied all of rotha for me. Now and forever, they were one and the same.

That night, he flopped on the urish, exhausted. I crawled beside him, propped up on an elbow, one leg atop his. We lay like that for a stupid long time, enjoying each other's company. A twitch in my chest made me physically jolt.

"I don't know what that was," I apologized. I didn't want him to think I had just passed gas in front of him.

It happened again.

"Is that the rotha like…kicking in?" I asked.

"Maybe you like me after all," he joked. His horn nuzzled my cheek.

I gave him a little push, but quickly melted back into him, snuggling close. I breathed in his scent.

"I love you, Katy," he murmured.

"I love you, Drex."

If I had thought the sex was amazing before, it had been nothing compared to that night we finally confessed our true desires for each other. We both had been holding back. I hadn't wanted to get too attached; he had kept his fating secret. I'd never connected so intensely or generously with someone. Something was freaking unlocked.

Chapter Thirty-Three
Home with You

Drex

I was met by two glasses on the urish table when I arrived home. One had a couple of swallows of fage, mine. Hers had been emptied. I drank my "shot" as she called them and ventured to the bedroom. For the last three days, she's been sprawled out on the bed, naked, and nearly panting for me. The days have been as intense as the nights. We haven't been able to get enough of each other. Already my cocks fill in anticipation.

Unlike yesterday, clothes didn't trail the floor. She kept me guessing. I positioned myself suggestively in the doorframe before opening it, hoping to impress her. Instead, I was surprised to find the bed made neatly—not rumpled with her waiting body. Still, she was up to *something*. I took off my gear—extra belts and the dagger I'd used to protect Katy. Nothing would protect her once I found her.

I glanced in the room that used to be hers. She'd been re-arranging it. I wasn't sure what her plans were for the room, but I had hopes it would be a nursery. I didn't feel rushed about it. It wasn't out of duty to my people anymore. It was about Katy. Katy wasn't going anywhere, no matter who came from the skies—humans from Earth, the shipbuilders themselves, or the wicked Orkain. Eventually, our growing love would manifest in little ones. I was ready to take whatever journey as long as it was with her.

There was only room left to search, the bathing room. I knocked. It would've been rude not to do so with the door shut. She drew my heart from my chest when she called out to me, "Come in, my Drex."

Hot steam billowed out as I made my way in. I closed the door behind me quickly. My cock thickened as I searched for my love, my vision obscured. I smelled hints of her, like honey notes dancing on the steam.

"Where are you, my Katy?" I asked.

I walked gingerly, careful not to slip since I was barefoot and the slate was wet. The shower was on recycle/steam but stood empty, creating the wonderful environment. I worked the buttons and removed my dampening pants as I searched for my woman. My long shirt draped over my cocks which reached in front of me, like a compass to the wet channels of my love. I reached the plunge pool, where she came into focus.

Katy stood at the edge of the pool where she had dipped with her clothes on. Below her shoulders, her hair hung wet around her. Her linen tunic refused to hang and drip, instead hugging the curves of her body. Her nipples were dark and sharp in the centers of her gorgeous breasts. The shirt clung to her belly and hips, showing off her full figure to me. It fell heavy in between her legs, exposing high thigh but hiding that wonderful triangle of sex. The back of the shirt was hiked atop her ass, water dripping down the round curves and the back of her legs. Stunning. I took her in with hungry eyes, my mouth agape.

I froze with all the possibilities. I wanted to start at her knees and lick all the way up to where her legs and ass meet, then wrap my tongue all along that edge of sexiness until I'd gotten a mouthful of butt cheek.

I wanted to put one of those linen-covered breasts in my mouth and suck until her legs rose to mount me. Then I wanted my cocks to enter the hidden area of her tunic and rub her until she moaned for me to be inside her.

I wanted to lift her and brace her up against the wall while my cocks explored deep inside her body. I want to stare into her eyes as I reached places no human could have pleased.

I wanted to do all of this, and more. I had a need to do these things. A thousand nights wouldn't touch what I wanted to do to her. She and this rotha were too much. It would kill me. I'd die trying to please her; a noble death to pursue. I'd collapse in between those breasts, worshiping this woman from the stars.

"Are you OK?" she barely hid her smile.

I gave a small nod, but to her, it probably seemed like a cry for mercy. She knew the effect she had on me. She seemed to delight in the power. My Katy was no longer shy. She knew exactly what she wanted and how to take it. It had left me breathless more than once.

She approached me with confident, swaying strides. My erect cocks determining the distance we kept. She closed my mouth with her delicate hand, and only then I realized it still hung open. Without breaking eye contact, she fell to her knees, a stack of towels supporting her and raising her so she could reach the base of my cock without me widening my stance.

She rolled the head of my cock in her mouth while her hands untangled my stems. Sucking the head was a tease. I wanted more of that soft, strong mouth. I inched my hips toward her but her elbows kept me deftly under control. Instead, she took to swallowing my cock tantalizingly slow, pulling my length into her with only the movement of her lips. With her back arched,

I had a perfect view of her ass. I brushed my fingers through the dry and wet lengths of her hair, massaging her head. I gathered her hair into my fist and wound it, pulling. Her hands worked my side cocks in rhythm with her mouth. I tried to be still as possible. It was worth it as she adjusted and took in more of me than I would think possible. My eyes rolled back in my head as her mouth hit the joint where my dicks met. Her forehead had made it against my stomach. It took all that was in me not to move. She was in control. I needed her permission. With her mouth and throat full of my cock, she fucking winked. It was too much; I knew what she wanted. My cock swelled and I kicked against the back of her throat.

The response was instantaneous. She gagged, her throat constricting around my cock as I pulled back. I convulsed dry as she coughed and sputtered. When I exited, her body remained ravenous. Her mouth was still open and greedy as she got off her knees. Her legs were slick with wetness.

She pulled off my shirt, damp with sweat, steam, and her saliva at its bottom edge. It was tossed to the floor. I peeled the wet tunic off her, revealing her silky skin. I picked her up, my arms under her ass and thighs, her sex on my belly, her tasty breasts between us. I kissed that mouth.

"What do you want?" I asked her hoarsely.

"I want *you*," she breathed into my ear, her arms pulling herself close, her breasts smashing into me.

In an instant, the steam became too much. She licked the lobe of my ear as I elbowed my way through doors and into the bedroom, where the rush of cool air teased our skin. She prickled up. Her nipples dug into me. I laid her on the bed and began kissing her dry. I would warm her against me.

"I want you," she breathed again.

I hid my smile against her body. She was asking for me. She would be begging by the time I would actually be inside her. I would see to that. She had teased me. I would tease her.

I kissed the tops of her breasts, between her breasts, round and round. I played with the edges of her perk peaks and I felt her squirm underneath me. When I finally took a nipple into my mouth, she grabbed my hair in wretched need. That's how it was going to be. Slow. Deliberate.

I pressed the joint of my tongues on the apex of her nipple. My tongues crept over her breast, pulling it into my mouth like tentacles on prey. I cupped the bare breast, so it was not neglected. It was heavy in my hand as I massaged it. Her hips and legs tilted and twisted toward me to remind me I could be doing other things while treating her breasts. I merely smiled with the bits of my mouth not working her tit. And dropped a heavy leg over her, anchoring her to the bed. She relaxed her hips back on the bed in simple resignation. She didn't know what she was in for.

When I had worked her nipple into a tense, sharp peak and reddened her skin with my sucking, I moved to her other breast. This one was just as sweet. Her skin was still damp, and her body warmed to my touch. I switched hands to tease the freshly sucked breast. When the sensitive skin jumped with my touch, I resigned to hold it stiffly instead. I brushed my teeth on her nipple. When I was satisfied that I'd treated them both equally, I propped them together and burrowed my tongue into her cleavage, popping out by her face—a preview for elsewhere.

I was on top of her now. She arched her back, a leg escaping and wrapping around me, trying to pull me in. I wouldn't have it; she was mine to tease. I flicked her nipples deftly with my thumb. Her head kicked back in response. I wished to kiss the jawline she presented with a million pecking kisses, but I'd made it this far and wouldn't backtrack. I recaptured her leg and made do by kissing the lines between breast and rib. I gathered flesh into my mouth, licking, kissing, biting. She inhaled with each sharp nibble, but otherwise tolerated my teasing. I kissed up and down her sides. I gave her belly button a little flick of my tongue, just another reminder of what awaited her soon.

I drew my fingers down her sides and reached her legs. Skipping over her sex, I started at her inner thighs, kissing near her knees. Her murmurs of pleasure had an air of frustration. She tried to draw me up with her feet, which was a fool's gesture at best.

I distracted her with a strum of my thumb on the lips of her pussy. Her hips jumped toward it; her body desperate for more. I returned to my previous engagement, kissing up one leg and then down the other.

Having given up hooking me with her legs, she lay back, panting with need. I had a perfect view between her open legs. My cocks had swollen so much they would no longer stay together. I wasn't sure who would give out on this teasing first. She was a soft and fragile thing. Every touch brought me pleasure.

"Please, Drex," she breathed, staring dead-eyed at the ceiling. I was at the other knee.

To hear her call my name was everything. I went up that leg a bit faster. My face once again reached her pussy. I breathed in her hot scent. I nosed her folds just barely before grazing my tongues across. Soft at first, hardly touching a thing. Katy had gone quiet, as if a noise might scare away all progress made. I didn't blame her. I had made her wait, and there was still more waiting to come. Her taste had changed with her delayed gratification. My tongue traced her edges, outlined her folds, wide-licked over her entrance. Two tongues pulled her wide as the third lolled over her clit in an arcing motion. It was more effective than I intended. The muscles in her legs tensed. I laid off, so she could come back to me. I didn't want her to orgasm yet. I wanted to be inside her first. A tongue would suffice. I plunged one into her sex.

"Oh, Drex."

Her channel rippled over me in pleasure.

Without a pause, I flicked my tongue in and out, while massaging her clit. She was quickly back on the edge. She grabbed a fistful of my hair, moaning and rocking. As she started toward what I knew would be her peak, my last tongue dove between her cheeks and tongued her asshole. Her entire body rolled into the orgasm. I almost came too. She cried out my name over and over as waves hit her. Hot cum coated my face as her body tensed, coiled, shuddered, and then plateaued.

I let up just so, keeping all the motions. She tried to back away from me, scoot away, her hands trying to find leverage with the sheets. My firm grip held her to my mouth. It was too much, too sensitive at first, so she fought, but I knew her body, in just a few moments, she'd go from tolerating to needing again if I just kept my mouth on her. I pushed my tongue gently into her channel, careful to avoid her G-spot. I kept my tongues on her clit and asshole. Her fighting turned to swaying her hips to encourage my tongue to reach her G-spot. I took the hint and gave it a shallow swipe. She murmured, and I did it again for her. Running on instinct, I slapped my tongue against it and held fast. Her hands immediately went to my horns as she screamed out, bucking violently against me. She was coming undone. Her orgasm flooded my mouth. I would gag on her pleasure. My cock dug into the mattress. When she finished, I was on top of her, my mouth still dripping with her taste.

"Yes, please," she requested.

I was so proud of her. I had teased her so much, then I'd made her cum twice, and she was still ready to take me in. Good. I needed her very wet and open for my cock. I separated my top cock and began massaging her clit. She put her hands on my arms on either side of her. "No, I want them all."

I could have milked right there. She wanted all of my cocks in her? I pulled them together again and tested it against her opening. It was small, and my penises only got wider past the head.

She nodded with wide eyes. "I want to try."

A devilish grin escaped my lips. My girl was always surprising me. I almost wished I wasn't as hard and needy as I was. I didn't want to hurt her. I nudged the head into her. She gasped for air, and her eyes rolled back in her head for a moment. Only at her opening, I could already tell her channel was clenching up on empty space. She was desperate for me. And I was desperate for her.

I monitored her face and her nails on my back. Every inch stretched her taut before she adjusted to accommodate me. I loved the tight, pulsating space. I struggled to remain in control.

I loved being completely inside her. I got on my elbows so we were face-to-face. I gently bit her lip, her ears. I'd never felt anything so intense. My dicks intertwined, inside her, exploring every bit of her cavity. She began breathing heavily, and I felt her core and channel tense with each pulse but never quite relax. She was building up, and that in turn was building me up. I couldn't catch my breath, my moment. Any baseline was dead and gone.

"Katy," I moaned into her ear.

"I know," she strained. "Me too. Come inside me, Drex. I want to feel you cum."

Her words were too much. I was ready to shoot from all my cocks.

"Are you sure?" I gasped; in a moment it would be too late to turn back.

"Yes!" she screamed as her moment began. Her hands dug into my back. The top half of her body lifted off the bed as her channel rippled around my cocks. "Come inside me, Drex!"

"Fryyre," I groaned as my cocks thrashed in her body. Her orgasm was so intense. I pushed deep inside as three jets of cum blasted her. With each pump of hot semen, she cried out, her core tensing to accept me and nearly pushing me out at the same time.

I felt another warmth. Checking, flame-shaped marks cradled Katy's belly as if I was pumping pure fire into her. They crept up her skin, dancing like electric pathways. She moaned in pleasure as they traveled around her breasts and up her collarbone. Katy gasped at the change in my appearance, unaware of her own.

We finished orgasming together. Her aftershocks tightened around my cocks creating confused waves of pleasure and sensitivity. The top half of her body met the bed again. We were both sweaty and sexy. Our hearts fluttered in unison. I listened to her try to catch her breath. When I had grown smaller, I slipped out of her. I moved beside her and pulled her close.

She raised her arms and admired her emblazoned body. She looked good in them. Now no one would question our togetherness, not even me.

"This is the rotha?" she asked.

"It's the markers for it, a manifestation of our togetherness and love. Rotha is our connection."

She traced the lines along my biceps as I held her.

"I love them," she said.

"I guess I did good." I joked as a way to ask for feedback. The sex had been intense and I wanted her to be comfortable with all of it, at all times.

"It was *so* good, Drex. And I'm going to lie here like this, as it's supposed to increase the chances. I don't know if it's true, but it can't hurt," she said, staying flat on her back.

My heart fluttered again in my chest. I propped myself up on an elbow so I could look into warm hazel eyes. This amazing woman. She wanted to be more than my lover, she wanted to be loved by me and to have my babies. Katy wanted to be with me, like this, and in so many other ways. She was my everything, not because I made her so, but because she wanted to be.

She giggled, embarrassed by the staring, and gave me a kiss. I kissed her back. We didn't move from there for a very long time. Something about increased chances, sure, but also because I couldn't imagine being anywhere better. She was my world.

Chapter Thirty-Four
Zarata

Katy

As I cleaned up, which included another shower, I admired the strokes of color which danced along my body. They loped along my belly and sides making me look thinner. They wrapped around my breasts, along my sternum, and tickled my collarbone. They crept down my arms ending on the backs of my hands. There was no texture, pain, or sensitivity. It was like they'd always been there. Maybe they had, and only now were brought forward. I wasn't sure how it worked, but I couldn't wait to show them off. My sister was my first call. I used the full-length settit in Drex's office. Sara took one look at the burnt sepia strokes along my upper body and jumped up and down for joy.

"I knew it! I knew it!" she shouted. "Dang, they're darker than mine," she cooed.

Her markings had grown farther up her arms and darker, since I'd last seen her.

"Did they just pop up? What were you doing?"

I scrunched my face up. I hadn't considered fielding that question. Suddenly that felt like a very personal question.

"Oh my god, Katy," she laughed, having figured it out on her own. "That instant, huh?"

I shrugged, relieved I wouldn't have to say it out loud. Rotha was a strange process.

My sister had been all good news as well. I got the feeling she'd been holding a lot back for my sake and now the floodgates opened. We were talking freely for the first time since maybe the Mike-pocalypse. She gushed and talked about all the things that had changed between her and Vance, including some things that were definitely Too Much Information, TMI, but I could tell she was excited to have someone to talk to about the changes she was going through. I was glad to get some insider information, too. I wished her the best in trying to get pregnant.

"Do you think men always show rotha signs first?" she asked.

"I don't know. Maybe now that we know we *can*, rotha will encounter less…resistance from us."

Vance came on screen to congratulate me, then Drex when I brought him over. I hoped Vance wouldn't connect our freshly showered markings with our sex as Sara had. Maybe I should have waited to call them.

"You are full of surprises, my man," he said to Drex. He was jovial and had the big smile on his face that he never seemed without. I had new respect for Vance now that I'd undergone my transformation. Sara was in good hands. Who knew we'd both find love across the galaxy. It was fate.

"We are having our kumirata tonight!" said Drex, pride ringing in his voice.

"Oh my gosh! Oh my gosh!" Sara fist-pumped the air. "Should I come over?"

"No," said Vance and Drex in unison, echoing my own. "Kumirata nights are sacred," we half-joked.

Truly, we didn't need to risk it again. And retaliation from the Orkain death wasn't out of the question.

#

The impromptu kumirata let everyone know the good news as soon as possible. Switching Day had started rumors about Drex and me. We wanted to squash them, but more so, we wanted to renew hope—that hope that had led them to agree to this unusual contract with the human species. There was rotha to be had, even if things were a bit more complicated than Sara's and Vance's experience seemed to present.

We sent out an announcement and everyone tuned in that evening to see our ceremony. I wore the dress from my showcase, sleeveless with a plunging neckline which now showed off my new sepia tones. He wore an open vest which showed off his markings as well, and some tight-fitting pants that showed off something else. We braided each other's hair, and I put small flowers into mine. He was so handsome. I was glad he was mine.

I didn't need decorations this time. I just needed him. I told him so in the vow I recorded. We stood in front of the camera, holding each other's hands. Our markers were so prominent. I loved them. We nervously fidgeted as our messages played for each other.

Mine: "I was lost, confused, and angry when I landed on Xavia. Truthfully, that wasn't a new state for me. I had been those things for years. You brought me in and despite what was at stake with your people, you were patient with me. I am forever grateful that you held my hand as I walked through that pain, so that we could be together now. I choose you. Forever."

Drex: "I've grown up under my parents' watchful eye—believing in rotha and its strong bond. I've grown up under the Orkain—desperate to save my people. However, it wasn't until I experienced rotha that I understood. Rotha will save us. Our bond, and the bonds Xavians build, will save our peoples. You make me stronger. I was a prince. Now I am a king. And you are my queen."

After our messages, we shared a very polite, royal kiss. After we shut off the cameras, we kissed another type.

"Are we really king and queen?" I asked.

"We are. You are." He smiled.

"I'm not sure if I'm ready for that."

"I am not worried. You would probably say you haven't been ready for anything you've tackled, and you've done so well. Besides, I knew you wanted a job."

I laughed. He was right. I already had so much planned. I was ready for at least the 'job' part of the job.

He touched the high of my cheek as the galaxies in his eyes glimmered. "I am so happy to have found you. I will never let you go."

I felt the same. Since letting myself love, I felt aligned with myself, with Drex, our hearts and souls— our zaratas. "You are my true love, my rotha."

I gave him a soft open kiss. His hand dropped to my lower back, receiving me.

"I love you," Drex said, his mouth against mine.

He scooped me up and carried me to our bed where he pleasured me until I was a soup of relaxation. Then he pulled me close to him and we fell asleep, our first kumirata night of all the nights to come. My life was just starting. The lines on my arms marked the way. I would no longer steer from them or run away. I had found my way, and it was in Drex's rotha drawn arms.

I hadn't expected to find love…anywhere, my planet or his. And now I'd found myself inextricably bound to the most perfect man. I had someone to love and care for me, and I to him. It was more than I'd dreamed, but who could've fathomed what lay beyond our stellar systems? I could only be grateful for whatever or however we came together. His people called it rotha. We didn't have a word for it. It was nothing like humans have experienced before. Perhaps if I was forced to choose a word, I'd choose *fate*.

Drex was my fate, but I had to choose him. I had to open myself up to him. And now I was loved in so many ways, and would love in so many ways to come.

Epilogue

Katy

My sister and Vance arrived at our door in the heat of the day. Knowing *how* to kill the Orkain was still far from being able to render them inert, and it was always safety first. Vance hovered around her like a worried gentleman. Sara laughed good-heartedly, having appeared to have indulged such things lately. Or, at least tolerated.

Sara looked wonderful. It might be her time in the sun, but she was glowing. I took her hands, looking her over, her marks darker than ever. Her bump was prominent on her frame. We shared smiles and giggles, then I gave her a big hug. Somehow Vance was able to get in through the door behind us. Drex gave him a hearty handshake. We finally got out of the doorway. And then Sara attacked the snacks. Even though it was later in the day, I still couldn't consider the thought of food. I had felt sick for several mornings now. I hoped I'd be able to return to eating again, soon.

Sara and Vance were here to announce their pregnancy to the Xavians officially, to confirm the rumors going around. It was like another kumirata, but much more casual. Still, I ushered Sara into our possible baby room so that we could do her hair. She wore a light blue silky dress that draped her belly beautifully. I French-rolled the hair on each side of her face and clipped it in the back. Her cheeks were red already. I added some glitter to her eyelids and her lips. She looked beautiful with just a few swipes of effort. She always did.

It was there I confided that I'd been sick for a few days. She put down her food plate and gave me a giant hug.

"Oh my gosh, sister!"

We both tried our hardest not to cry off the makeup we had put on.

"Who would have imagined?" I laugh-cried.

"That we'd both find our true loves and be pregnant with their babies? Not I."

"Not me, either."

"They'll be close to the same age, like we were. They'll be so close!" Sara hugged me and threatened to upturn her hair I just styled.

We composed ourselves and came back out. Sara refilled her food plate. I tested out a cracker-like thing called a brack. My stomach didn't complain too much, but I still handed the rest to Drex.

He bit his lip. "Are you OK?" he whispered.

Before I could even answer, he took me by the hand and pulled me into the privacy of the kitchen. Despite confessing my morning sickness to my sister, we still hadn't said out loud what my sickness could mean. He suspected what I suspected as well. There weren't any pregnancy tests here, so we just had to wait it out. He kissed my hairline and held me close, his hand dangerously close to tangling in my hair at the nape of my neck.

"I'm OK," I assured him.

His body grazed mine as he dropped to his knees. It sent a shiver up my spine, his face so close to my waist. I knew it was just a tease though. I refused the temptation of putting my hands in his freshly coiffed hair.

He had another goal in mind. He put his mouth to my belly and whispered a secret to our possible little one. He came back up the way he went down, dangerously close to my cleavage, breathing heat into my dress.

"What did you tell my tummy?" I asked, still not ready to describe it as a baby.

"That they're going to be raised by the queen and king of a united people. They'll grow strong and safe, and wrapped in a binding, rotha love that you taught me." His eyes were deep and intense.

I gave him another kiss, because if I listened to any more of his confident words, I would cry. The hormones must be getting to me, and we had duties to attend to.

There were so many things that needed to be done, and so we wanted to get this one off the list. After our kumirata, I wanted to help the Xavians and my fellow humans work together. It was funny. In denying myself, I was denying a lot of good, too. After making my decision, I found myself able and ready to help others. It turned out it wasn't a selfish or foolish choice. I wanted to help make Xavia safer and more comfortable for everyone.

We now knew how to kill the Orkain, and so we could fight back and live more safely and freely. There was discussion of waging war, developing weapons, and even eradicating them from the planet. It was drastic, but they were hunting the Xavians into extinction. If the Xavians wanted to endure, they needed to fight back.

But for now, we were fighting back with love, and loved ones, and new little ones.

"As Queen and King of your united people, we are happy to announce the pregnancy of two of our closest friends and family—Vance and Sara."

Drex and I stepped away so that the cameras could see Vance and Sara behind us. Vance had a grin that threatened to take over his face. He had an arm around small Sara who was absolutely glowing with her own giant smile. She waved at the camera with her best beauty pageant wave, the other hand on her unmistakable belly.

I took in the audience on the settit, human and Xavian. There was still so much unknown, but here was unmistakable hope. This was everyone's new beginning, not just for humans who had traveled across the galaxy; not just for the remaining Xavians who had just figured out how to fight back against their vicious enemies, but for all of us. There had been a lot stacked against us, but we were choosing love, hope, and new beginnings. I couldn't wait to see what our families would accomplish next.

In a not very kinglike fashion, Drex stepped behind me and hugged me. In that moment, he wasn't my king. He was my lover, my friend, father of my children, and my rotha. My Xavian King would always be my Xavian Prince.

Free Bonus Scene

Haven't gotten enough of Katy and Drex?

Download a free bonus scene, *Katy and Drex Try 69*, as a special gift when you sign up for my newsletter, Reverie's Reveries.

Reverieharwood.com/newsletter-prince

A Note for You, the Reader

Hi Reader,

Thank you so much for taking a chance on me, Katy, Drex, and *Rotha Mates of Xavia*.

The first manuscript I ever completed as a young middle-school writer was a romance. I've now returned to the stories that intrigued me, made me cry, and made me hopeful.

A special thank-you to advanced readers for their kind feedback which sent this book through a whirlwind revision prior to its full release. This book is better because of you.

I hope *My Alien Prince* has added romance and steaminess…and, a little escape…to your day. Join me for the next adventure, *My Alien Protector* coming soon.

What did you think of Drex and the Xavian world? Send me an email at reverie@reverieharwood.com. If you like booktok or cats, you can follow me on TikTok @reverieharwood. No matter how you reach out, I'd love to hear from you.

Until then, my very best to you,

Reverie Harwood
February 2023

www.ingramcontent.com/pod-product-compliance
Lightning Source LLC
Chambersburg PA
CBHW051252210726
48287CB00002B/468